Praise for Pamela Fryer's
The Midnight Effect

"Pamela Fryer's smooth, unobtrusive writing style adds to the enjoyment of this fascinating story ... GOOD READING!"

~ *Long and Short Reviews*

"TOP Notch storytelling! I am looking forward to more books by Ms. Fryer!"

~ *Single Title Reviews*

"I loved The Midnight Effect. It was a pitch-perfect page turner with a likable hero, heroine and child! The characters were well-motivated and stayed in character and the complicated plot was fleshed out flawlessly."

~ *Night Owl Romance Reviews*

The Midnight
Effect

Pamela Fryer

A SAMhAIN pUbLIShING, LTO. publication.

Samhain Publishing, Ltd.
577 Mulberry Street, Suite 1520
Macon, GA 31201
www.samhainpublishing.com

The Midnight Effect
Copyright © 2010 by Pamela Fryer
Print ISBN: 978-1-60504-746-1
Digital ISBN: 978-1-60504-656-3

Editing by Heidi Moore
Cover by Natalie Winters

First Samhain Publishing, Ltd. electronic publication: August 2009
First Samhain Publishing, Ltd. print publication: June 2010

Dedication

To a real hero who cooks and cleans and does his own laundry so I have time to write. These are the very least of the reasons I love you so much. And of course to my writer friends in the San Francisco Area RWA; it is because of your support that I made it this far. Jennifer, you especially.

Chapter One

Miles Goodwin tipped his chair back as he took a slug from his beer. Across the tree line the remainder of the day was a bloody smear on the horizon. The setting sun drifted away mockingly. *Another day and you're still here because you don't have the courage to put your revolver in your mouth.*

He smacked at a mosquito on his neck. The bugs were relentless at dusk, but this was Miles' favorite time of day. Swallowing darkness was moments away, when he wouldn't recognize each agonizing minute in the passage of time. Night was limbo in the personal hell his life had become.

It was a chore to drag himself out of bed every morning, painful to endure every endless minute. The mark of each sunset brought him one day closer to the end he longed for. Closer to the end he didn't have the courage to seek on his own. Suicide was a sin, and if there was a sweet hereafter, he wouldn't join Sara and Michelle there if he took his own life.

The roar of an engine pulled his attention to the dark tunnel of Northern pine where the highway wound out of sight. The front legs of his chair fell onto the porch with a *thunk*. He rarely saw a customer at his little gas station after six. By now most of the tourists were already in town at the expensive restaurants, sipping their second martinis.

A classic Mercedes two-seater raced around the bend and

went into a drift on squealing tires.

The car fishtailed before regaining traction. Clouds of white smoke poured from the exhaust as though it had blown a head gasket. As it barreled down the highway at breakneck speed, chunks of rubber flapped at the right rear wheel. The car was out of control, but the driver wasn't trying to stop.

Sparks flew from the rim as the last shreds of the tire disintegrated. The car careened down the embankment on the side of the highway and launched off the incline, headed directly for his small station.

"Jesus!" Miles leapt to his feet and dove off the porch, narrowly missing the rusted edge of a twisted bumper as he hit the ground. He scrambled to his feet and ran, still clutching his foaming beer bottle, as the car crashed into the pumps.

A dull *whuff* pressed on his eardrums as the pumps exploded. For the space of a heartbeat the dusky forest was as bright as high noon.

Miles hit the emergency shut-off lever at the side of the garage and the tanks sealed off, but the car was already on fire. There were no sprinklers at the historic station's stand-alone island.

Nobody could have lived through an explosion like that. At that horrific moment, he knew there was at least one dead body at Goodwin's Garage.

The irony hit him—there could have been two. What had made him run? He'd been longing for death for three years, aching for it more with each day that passed. Yet at the first sign of danger he'd been on his feet, preserving his sorry ass. It had been instinct as much as police training.

Dammit to hell.

Momentum had taken the car past the worst of the flames. The windshield was a shattered milky spider web, but still held.

Conditioned by police training, he ran toward the car without thinking, more concerned for the driver than for himself.

Movement shifted behind the white-green kaleidoscope of safety glass. A hand passed over the steering wheel, and Miles knew it was a woman in the car.

She's alive—there must be a God in heaven.

The driver's door opened as flames burst across the hood. She staggered out and fell to her knees.

A second explosion rocked the quiet mountainside. Still running, Miles threw up his arm to block the intense heat.

His heart caught in his throat as he rounded the coupe's door and saw she had a little girl clutched under her arm.

The woman braced herself on the ground with her other hand as she tried to get away from the burning car. He grabbed her by the forearm and hauled her to her feet. She wobbled unsteadily as he pulled her arm over his shoulder. The child scrambled past him, headed for the backside of his garage.

A confusing mixture of past and present rocked him like a punch to the gut. She wasn't his beloved daughter, but the sight of her blond hair tossing as she ran ahead of him sent coherence spinning away.

The woman moaned and her weight sagged on him, bringing him back to the here and now.

"Help..."

He dragged her away from the car. "Jesus, lady, what the hell? Are you trying to get killed?"

He was practically carrying her by the time they arrived at the corner of the building where the little girl waited, shielded from the scorching heat.

"Aunt Lily!" She threw her arms around her aunt's waist.

The woman knelt and gripped the child by her shoulders. "Are you okay?"

She nodded, sniffing.

"I'm so sorry." She pulled the child close. "It's okay, Annie. We're going to be okay."

"Not if you keep driving like that," Miles growled. "You just blew up my gas station."

The woman glanced at him. The horror in her eyes made him flinch. A trickle of blood ran down her temple and spattered her blouse.

"You're hurt," Annie said. Her voice trembled with the precursor to tears. She reached out and touched the woman's face with tiny, hesitant fingertips. The gesture caused his shriveled heart to jerk.

Without removing those wide, brown eyes from his, Lily took her niece's hand and stood. Only then did she glance past him.

"Is that your truck?"

His mouth fell open. "Lady, you need an ambulance."

Would the phone still work, or had the destruction of his station knocked out power and phone lines? Services were finicky enough up here without being rocked by a two-megaton blast.

"He's coming," Annie whimpered.

The horror in Lily's eyes deepened. She glanced at the child and started past him.

"I need your vehicle."

Before he could have guessed this night would get any weirder, she snatched up a rusted sliver of metal and whirled around, pointing it at him.

"Give me the keys."

She's robbing me with an old antenna? "You've got to be kidding."

"Aunt Lily," Annie persisted with greater urgency.

Slivers of wood exploded from the corner of the building above his ear. Miles heard the muffled chirp over the roar of the fire. He knew what it was even before a second shot whizzed past his head. The sound sent him careening back to his eight years with the Seattle PD.

Silencer.

Chapter Two

Lily gasped as wood chips sprayed over her. In the shadows of the darkening forest, she saw Colton's assassin advancing on the burning station. He'd left his SUV on the side of the highway, driver's door standing open.

"Mister, we need to get out of here *now*."

The gas station attendant was already moving, already sifting through the ring of keys clipped to his belt. With the other hand, he seized her forearm and dragged her along.

Her legs were wobbly and her body wouldn't respond to the commands her brain was sending. None of this seemed real. It felt more like a bad movie on a television with only one channel.

She struggled against him, trying to shield Annie while somewhere in the back of her mind she knew it wasn't Annie that Colton's assassin was trying to kill.

The station attendant opened the driver's door, scooped Annie up and tossed her inside. Lily's foot slipped on the tall truck's chrome stirrup. He caught her around the waist, shoved her in with one hand on her rear and leapt in behind her.

He slotted and turned the key. The engine came to life with a throaty roar.

Hurry, hurry, hurry, she wanted to yell, but didn't have the breath to manage the words.

A shot shattered the driver's window and punched a hole in the windshield as it exited. Annie screamed. Lily looked out the rear window to see the shooter walking casually toward them, eerily silhouetted by the licking orange inferno behind him.

Their rescuer dumped the clutch and wrenched the wheel, rocketing the truck into a spin and spraying a wave of gravel over their attacker. While fumbling with the seatbelt, she glanced out again to see Colton's assassin recoil from the rocks. The muzzle of his gun flashed white as he squeezed off a wild shot.

"Hold on," the man said, almost too calmly.

Lily wrapped her arms around her niece. The truck had a customized interior with two deep bucket seats. No safe place for Annie to sit.

The man launched them over the plateau behind the station and down toward a valley of black pine. The radio blared, churning out rock 'n roll. He shut it off.

"All right lady, who wants you dead?"

Lily gripped the passenger handle as he tore through a fallen log like it was tissue paper. "Shouldn't you turn on the lights?"

All she needed was for him to slam into a tree. Colton's henchman had been driving a luxury SUV. It wasn't equipped for this kind of hard four-wheeling, but she wouldn't put it past him to try and follow.

"I know where I'm going."

This isn't happening.

She chewed her bottom lip. "I'm so sorry." Only after she'd said it did she realize how ridiculous her apology sounded. Her brain was functioning on overload and she almost didn't believe they had escaped.

We haven't. Colton Reilly will find us. It's only a matter of time.

Annie wriggled in her lap. "Where are we going, Aunt Lily?"

"To the police station," the man answered for her.

"No!" Lily jerked upright. "Look, I'll pay for the damage, but you can't take us to the police. We haven't committed a crime. She won't be safe there."

"In case you haven't noticed, someone is shooting at you." He growled the words with sarcasm, as if she were too stupid to realize it. "You need help."

"Yeah, I do. But I'm not going to get it from some two-bit hillbilly cop."

"You're looking at a two-bit hillbilly cop, lady."

Lily's heart gave a painful kick. How much worse could her luck get?

"I'm not active," he clarified almost reluctantly. "I'm on leave from Seattle PD."

He righted the wheel as the truck lurched over a ravine. How could he navigate through this darkness? She screamed as a pine bough struck the windshield in front of her face.

He turned the truck onto a fire road and Lily drew a relieved breath as the ride became smoother.

The man was pissed off, and rightfully so. She'd destroyed his garage and nearly killed him. But there had to be a way to appeal to him. He was good looking enough. Maybe she could seduce him into letting her go?

Right. She was a computer nerd, not a seductress. Besides, he was a cop. He'd seen and heard it all.

"I'm really sorry about your station. I didn't mean to hit it, but he'd shot my tire out and I lost control."

"I'll say."

"Please, don't take us to the police station. It's the first place he'll look. We need to go someplace he can't track us."

He tossed a wary glance her way. Was her voice soft enough, her eyes pleading enough? *Try harder, Lily. Annie's safety and your very life depend on it.*

If he took them to the police station, it was all over. Colton Reilly would waltz in with his money and his lawyers, and she would be escorted away in handcuffs.

"Please. I'll pay you twice what your station was worth."

"I don't give a crap about that dump. I have insurance."

She was making a mess of this like she made a mess of everything. She smoothed Annie's silken blond hair. Her niece looked up at her with terrified eyes, rendering Lily mute.

I'm sorry, Annie. I don't know how to be a mommy. I don't know how to keep you safe.

"I'll make you a deal." He blasted an angry sigh, as though on the brink of changing his mind. "You tell me who that was, and I'll take you somewhere safe."

Hope blossomed in her chest. But could she trust him?

He carefully angled the truck around a sharp bend in the dirt road. He looked at her when she remained silent.

"He works for Annie's father."

He rolled his eyes. "Shit."

"Her father is Colton Reilly."

The man frowned. "Colton Reilly, the loony scientist from Intelli something?"

"IntelliGenysis," she confirmed, even though scientist was the wrong way to describe him. From what Lily had learned in the last few days, Colton Reilly was more of a cultist whose operation read like a John Grisham novel. In recent months, mysteriously   disappearing   personnel   and   questionable

15

experiments within the sealed-up research facility had caught the attention of the FBI.

She hoped the ex-cop had heard the same things.

"Mister, please," Annie whimpered.

His gaze flicked over and fell on Annie. He clenched his jaw and his Adam's apple rose and fell.

"Ah, Christ."

Miles angled the truck around the backside of the cabin. As soon as he turned the engine off, Annie started shrieking.

"Aunt Lily, wake up! Aunt Lily, please!"

The woman sagged against the door, eyes closed. The blood dripping down her temple had soaked the shoulder of her blouse.

Miles jumped out and ran to the passenger door. He caught Lily as she slumped toward him. He reached over and released the seatbelt, and she fell into his arms.

Emotions stabbed him like lightning strikes. He hadn't touched another woman since Sara's death. Hadn't even stood close enough to touch one.

Annie jumped out behind her, apparently none the worse for wear. *Thank God.*

He cradled Lily against his chest, too aware of the softness of her body and the light scent of flowers coming from her hair. The danger had left a wild feeling in his gut, but being so close to this woman was what brought on the nausea.

Dammit, I don't need this.

Touching her brought back memories he'd rather have left dead. It was absurd. Lily meant nothing to him and there was no reason he couldn't carry her to safety, but he'd wound himself into his numb cocoon so tightly it hurt to come out.

He hefted her up and fumbled for the key to the cabin with one hand.

"Can you unlock the door, sweetie?"

Annie took the key he'd singled out and ran ahead to the door. Her little Sesame Street sneakers made hollow thumps on the porch steps.

She pushed the door open but didn't go inside. "It's dark. I don't like the dark."

"It's okay, sweetheart. I'll put on a light." He angled past her and eased Lily onto the couch.

The woman turned her head and her eyes fluttered. "Mmm. Cassie."

Miles hit the light switch by the door. The bulb in the lamp flashed and burned out. Annie gave a fearful squeak. He crossed to the kitchen and flipped on the work light over the stove. Dingy yellow light pooled in the tiny kitchen and strayed into the cabin's family room. Only then did Annie step through the doorway. Miles moved around her to close the door, constantly watched by her wide eyes.

He mustered a smile. It felt odd on his face.

Miles considered his approach. He'd almost forgotten how to talk to a child. Thank God, he'd had little practice talking to a frightened one. Until the day she'd died, his daughter's greatest fears had been imaginary monsters under the bed.

He opened his mouth to speak, but decided on a different tactic. He turned to the dresser unit against the wall and pulled open the top drawer. His mouth went dry. The black leather wallet was still there.

Of course it was. Where would it go? He flipped it open. His badge had tarnished. The face in the ID photo looked twenty years younger. Fitting. He felt twenty years older.

He knelt in front of the frightened little girl and forced another stiff smile.

"Annie, my name is Miles Goodwin. I'm a police officer."

"Is Aunt Lily going to be okay?"

He nodded, even though he wasn't entirely sure. Head injuries were always an uncertainty. "I'm going to take good care of you both. I know someone very bad is trying to hurt Lily."

Annie chewed her lower lip. He showed her his badge.

"I work for a big police station in the city. There are lots of policemen there who can help keep you safe. But I have to ask you a question, and it's really important you give me an honest answer. Okay?"

"'kay."

"Did Lily take you away without permission?"

Annie shook her head.

"How come you're with your aunt instead of your father?"

"Because the lady from the office said so."

"What lady?"

Annie returned a blank stare like all kids did when they didn't know what was going on. Fair enough. New tactic.

"Is Lily nice to you?" Talking to a little girl felt foreign, almost like a betrayal to his daughter's memory. He ground his teeth and swallowed against the sourness rising in his throat.

Annie nodded. "She's my mommy's sister."

"Where's your mommy?"

"In heaven. Aunt Lily says it's a good place."

Miles took a deep, shuddering breath. "And your daddy, what's he like?"

She pouted. "He puts me in the water. Please don't make

me go back there. I don't like it there. Please, it's a bad place. They make us do bad things."

Annie's face scrunched up like she was going to cry. Her desperation squeezed at his heart.

"I won't make you do anything you don't want to do, except eat your vegetables."

The kid didn't even crack a smile. No wonder, considering. After he said it, it sounded dumb even to him.

"I'm going into the bathroom to get some bandages. Wait right here, okay? Don't go anywhere."

"I won't."

He retrieved the first-aid kit under the sink, hoping the woman wouldn't need stitches. The wound at her head was bleeding badly, but butterfly tapes would have to do.

Miles sat on the edge of the tired, old couch while Annie shyly explored the main room.

Eddie had kept the place neat, but Miles could tell the retired cop had taken special care not to change a thing. All of it was exactly as he remembered...too well.

He unzipped the folding kit and laid it open. Lily stirred but didn't open her eyes. He soaked a cotton swab with antibacterial cleanser and leaned over to reach the wound on her head. His hip made contact with hers, sending his emotions out of control. She was soft and feminine and utterly helpless.

Dammit, he didn't like these reminders he was still a man, still alive. He would give anything to crawl back into his self-inflicted emotional coma and be left alone.

But at the same time, he couldn't turn a blind eye to this situation. His police training wouldn't allow him, nor would the man he used to be.

If only this hadn't happened to a beautiful woman and a

19

golden child, it would be easier to step into his old role.

Miles touched Lily's cheek and turned her face. Her skin was soft and supple, a foreign thing under his fingers. She moaned and shifted, pinching her brow. He swabbed gently with the antibacterial. Her lips parted and she caught a sharp breath as the stinging ointment touched the wound. She shifted on the couch and tried to move away.

"Easy now," he said. "It only hurts for a second." He touched her cheek again, preventing her from turning away.

He leaned over and reached with the cotton. His forearm came into contact with the lush swell of her breast. Miles jerked back, stunned and ashamed of the electric zing racing through him. He swallowed past the sudden dryness in his mouth and reached again, more carefully this time.

Miles swabbed the cut clean and closed it up with two butterfly tapes. They didn't stick well to her hair, but the wound wasn't as bad as he'd first thought. She'd be on her feet, and more importantly, on her way, first thing in the morning.

Thank God. He would pretend none of this ever happened.

In his peripheral vision he saw Annie hesitantly exploring the cabin. She stopped at the half-wall dividing the kitchen from the small family room and bent to retrieve something that had fallen behind the credenza there.

She'd found Michelle's Tigger the Tiger doll. Annie held the stuffed toy in her hand and picked a dust bunny off its paw.

A bittersweet ache swept over him so powerfully he nearly cried out. Michelle had been heartbroken when the toy went missing. He wanted to scream at Annie to put it down, but his jaw was locked and his breath cut off.

The rational part of him knew Annie was just a frightened little girl and there was no reason to punish her for touching a stuffed toy. The irrational part of him saw the Tigger as one last graspable piece of his daughter that hadn't been stolen from him.

Annie looked up, her face an angelic vision of innocence in its purest form. "What happened to her?"

A chill rolled over his flesh. His dead heart struggled to beat. "She... There was an accident."

Annie set the doll down carefully on top of the credenza and arranged it in a sitting position. Her fingers combed the orange fluff of its forelock straight up. She turned and walked toward him, smiling. "You were a good dad."

Miles couldn't draw a breath. The eeriness of her words was forgotten for the crippling sadness squeezing the life out of him.

He hadn't talked about Michelle to anyone since her death. Had never said those words aloud before.

My wife and daughter died in a car crash.

The people in town knew what had happened and never spoke about it. Those who knew him well smiled uncomfortably and intentionally brought up mundane topics. Those who didn't looked at him with pitying eyes and didn't talk at all.

Annie dropped to her knees beside the couch and placed both hands on Lily's forearm. "Aunt Lily?"

The woman shifted and opened her eyes. "I'm here, honey."

"Are you okay?"

"I bumped my head a little too hard."

Miles stood and stalked to the kitchen. The tenderness they displayed for each other was too much for him to bear. He braced both hands on the counter, but his eyes strayed back to them against his will.

In the fifteen minutes since they'd careened into his life, he'd been a different man than the one who had drifted aimlessly for the last three years. He'd risen each day, shaved and eaten three meals, but he hadn't been alive. He'd existed in despair, dulled to emotion and sensation and thought.

Now his pulse was racing, and he felt like he'd just come off a training maneuver. His every sense was on high alert. That had to be why, when he looked into Lily's warm brown eyes, he couldn't remember the last time he'd seen such a beautiful woman.

Not since Sara.

Miles swallowed past the choking realization. *I can't do this. I'm not the man I used to be.*

Lily turned onto her side and hugged Annie.

"I'm scared," Annie said in a tiny voice.

Lily's deep brown gaze found him. "Shh. I know. It's going to be all right."

Miles withered under those soft, doe eyes. He turned and ran a hand through his hair. His stomach grumbled. He hadn't had dinner yet, but it was the excitement that had left him ravenous.

Without speaking, he opened a can of beef stew and dumped it into a saucepan. He rifled through the cabinets. Eddie had promised to keep the cabin stocked even though Miles had assured him he didn't care, the cabin was his now. It held too many painful memories for Miles to ever enjoy being here again.

He found a tube of biscuits in the freezer and used a can opener to remove both aluminum ends before sticking it in the microwave to defrost, then turned on the electric oven.

In the fifteen minutes it took to prepare their meager meal, the silence was painful.

He looked over at his guests. Annie had moved into the

spot on the edge of the couch he'd vacated. She touched her aunt's cheek with one hand. Another eerie sensation washed over him and he thought back to her uncanny statements. The way she sat now, one palm against her aunt's head, was almost purposeful.

What had made her think Miles had a little girl? A Tigger doll could appeal to a boy as much as a girl. And what on earth made her think Michelle was gone? Was his despair etched so deeply in his face even a child could read it?

Annie leaned back. She looked over at Miles, and then to the two bowls he'd filled on the counter.

"Are you hungry?"

She nodded.

He grinned. It still felt odd, wrong even, but it was getting easier. "Well, come on."

She hopped off the couch and skipped over to the table as happily as a girl scout at a picnic. He set a bowl before her then went to the couch and knelt beside Lily. She watched him cautiously.

"Whose cabin is this?"

"Mine."

She sat up. "We aren't safe here." Lily swayed and placed her fingertips to her temple. He steadied her with a hand on her shoulder and just as quickly jerked away. Each touch of her warm, feminine softness sent a bolt of electricity racing through his nerve endings. She reminded him what a woman felt like. That he *enjoyed* what a woman felt like.

He had to get rid of her, pronto.

"Take it easy. The deed is in a friend's name. No one knows I own the place."

She pressed the back of her hand to her forehead and let

out a long breath.

"Can you eat?"

Her stomach growled. He took it as a yes. "It isn't much."

She touched his arm. The contact was another lightning strike to senses that wanted to be left numb.

"I can't tell you how sorry I am."

"That's not what I want you to tell me."

She met his gaze. God, she was a beautiful woman, and those melted-chocolate eyes threatened to drown him.

"I want the truth."

Chapter Three

An explanation was the least she owed him. She had destroyed his business and risked his life, involving him in something that should have been her problem alone.

At the same time, Lily didn't like being treated like a criminal. She'd heard him ask Annie if she was taken without permission. His suspicion added insult to the astronomical injury she'd experienced over the last three days.

But Lily bit her lip as she sat at the table opposite Annie and picked up her spoon. She needed him. Without this man's help she had nothing. Her transportation, and her evidence, had just been destroyed in a flaming inferno.

Miles ate in the kitchen. He alternated between tidying up and spooning stew into his mouth over the sink. Lily saw it for what it truly was—avoidance. For some reason he was uncomfortable around her.

Was it because he suspected her of committing a crime? She supposed it was cop detachment. He didn't want to become friendly with her if there was a chance he would have to slap her in cuffs.

"It's good," Annie said, beaming. Lily laughed. As bad as their situation was, Annie was a beacon of light. Lily had only known her niece three days, but already she couldn't imagine life without her.

Annie was as puzzling as their mysterious savior. When the social worker had produced her, the little girl was wearing an olive green suit almost like hospital scrubs, and plain slip-on sneakers. She hadn't known what a hamburger was. She had never watched *Sesame Street*.

She was not your ordinary six-year-old.

At first Lily had thought her quiet reservation was from the shock of losing her mother and shyness at meeting a new person whom she was told, by yet another stranger, would be her new mommy. But then glimpses of Annie's remarkable uniqueness began to slip through. She was twice as intelligent as the average six-year-old and eerily mature.

Lily looked up in time to see the man glance away quickly. He turned his back and washed out the pot he'd used to heat the stew.

"You didn't tell me your name," she said gently.

His attention jerked. It almost seemed he didn't want to.

"Miles. Goodwin."

Lily noticed it then, a stuffed Tigger the Tiger doll on the credenza behind Annie. She should have realized he had his own family. She'd nearly killed him earlier today. Nearly made a widow out of his wife and orphans out of his children.

She glanced up and found his eyes boring into her. "I'm Lily." Her voice came out a whisper.

He didn't respond as he cleared away their bowls and started to wash them.

"Can I help?" she asked.

"No need."

Annie scooted out of her chair. She hugged Lily around the waist. "That was good. What was it called?"

"It was beef stew."

"I like beef stew."

"Me too. It's yummy." She smiled at her precious niece and then glanced up to find a disbelieving expression on Miles' face. She would have to explain what she knew about Annie, too.

He wiped his hands on a towel, and his expression turned to something bordering disapproval. He was an incredibly handsome man, but his eyes were edged with sorrow that seemed permanently fixed there.

"The bathroom is in back. You can take the bedroom tonight."

It would be stupid to argue. She and Annie couldn't both take the couch and issuing frivolous protests would only be rude.

"Thank you."

She took Annie by the hand and led her into the bedroom as Miles knelt at the credenza and retrieved a radio handset. His gaze landed on the doll and froze there for a long moment.

Annie went into the bathroom as Lily turned down the bed. It was a queen, and the sheets appeared freshly changed. Still, she wondered if she'd be able to sleep.

She had known from the start she would have to hire a lawyer and expected an ugly court battle. But never in her wildest dreams did she expect Colton Reilly would try to kill her.

None of the witnesses to her sister's accident had been able to recall any important details. Cassie had insisted on making the video for Lily, but had died before giving details of her hit-and-run. Was it possible her sister's death wasn't a tragic accident as the police in Spokane suspected, but something more sinister?

In the other room the radio crackled with static. She heard

the words "fire" and "gas station," as Miles listened to the police band, but nothing about the shooter. She knew Colton's henchman was smart enough not to wait around to get caught.

Lily sat on the edge of the bed and leaned her elbows on her knees, rubbing her face. She was bone weary and didn't have the slightest idea what she was going to do.

A week ago her life was normal. Happy. She had a thriving business and a gorgeous townhouse in Seattle's expensive Rose Crest development.

Then, in the span of two days, she'd received two life-changing blows. Her sister had died. And she was the guardian of the niece she never even knew she had.

"What time does she go to bed?"

Lily tensed. Miles stood in the doorway. His expression held forbidding suspicion.

Lily glanced at the clock. It was eight fifteen. "I'll put her to bed early. I know you'll want to get home to your family as quickly as possible."

"No need." He looked away and his Adam's apple bobbed. "My wife and daughter..." His voice cracked with emotion so powerful she felt it in her own heart.

She understood. The pain in his eyes had been put there.

"Don't—" He held up a hand. "Don't say you're sorry."

She glanced at the floor, not sure what to say at all.

"You might find some clothes..." he trailed off. "I'd prefer if you didn't wear them."

"All right."

He scowled, wiping the sadness from his face, and crossed the small bedroom with severe steps. Miles opened the closet and pulled a flannel button-up shirt from a hanger. His gaze fell on the blood stain on her blouse as he tossed the shirt onto the bed beside her.

"You'll need something more. Could get cold."

"Thank you."

"I think there's a new toothbrush in the bathroom. Help yourself to whatever you find there."

She nodded, but he'd already turned away.

Annie bounded out of the bathroom. "There's a shower in there like in the hotel room."

Lily smiled as she scooped her up and sat her down on the bed. "It's been a really scary day, hasn't it?"

Annie's exuberance faded and she nodded.

"Tomorrow we're going to go to the police in Seattle and they're going to protect us."

"What if he finds us before then?"

It wasn't the first time she noticed Annie didn't refer to Colton Reilly as "Daddy". Lily slipped off the bed to kneel in front of Annie and unlace her new sneakers.

"He won't. He doesn't know where we've gone now, and you need a special car to get here."

"Like Mr. Miles'?"

"Yep." Lily tried to keep an upbeat expression, but feared Annie saw right through it. "I know it's earlier than you usually go to bed, but I need to go talk to Mr. Miles."

"Okay." Annie flopped down on the pillow. "I'm tired anyway." The impish grin she offered reached right into Lily's heart and squeezed.

"Me too. I'll back in a little while." She didn't need to ask if Annie wanted the light left on. She wasn't just afraid of the dark, she was terrified.

"Aunt Lily?"

"Yes, sweetie?" Lily pulled the covers up and sat on the edge of the bed.

"What's that sound?"

"What sound?" Worry stabbed the pit of her stomach. Was this another example of the child's odd intuitiveness?

Annie turned her head toward the window. "That one."

Relief washed over Lily like a tidal wave. After what she'd been through today, there wasn't much more she could withstand. "Those are crickets. They're pretty bugs who sing in the night."

"Why?"

"To help little girls fall asleep, that's why." Lily managed a smile and tweaked Annie's nose. "Try to get some rest, okay?"

Annie giggled. "'kay."

Lily took the shirt Miles gave her and went into the bathroom. She removed her ruined blouse and slipped into the fuzzy flannel. His scent wrapped around her like a warm blanket, reassuring and masculine. The simple traces made her feel safe, protected. Lily frowned at her pathetic reflection in the mirror. Nothing could be further from the truth.

After washing out her blouse in the sink, she walked softly through the bedroom and eased the door closed. Her hands shook as she crossed the cabin's small living room. She wondered how best to present her wretched tale without coming off like a nutcase.

Miles sat at the table watching her with a scrutinizing gaze. "Local boys are all over what's left of my station. Your friend's long gone. My guess is he's waiting for me to turn you over to the police."

She sat across from him and folded her hands together on the table.

"I'm taking you to Seattle tomorrow. My sergeant is the right man to help, if your story checks out."

His statement was a warning, ringing loud and clear. *If your story checks out.*

"You might as well tell me first. You'll need someone in your corner."

She glanced up. Was he that person? She wasn't certain. Miles' eyes were hard and his expression severe.

Tragedy had etched deep lines around vibrant blue eyes, but his thick, dark hair didn't possess a hint of gray. He had the rugged good looks of a man who preferred the mountains to the city.

"You should go to the police here in town, tell them I robbed you and stole your truck."

He scowled. "Not only would that make me a laughing stock, nobody would believe it. I have a black belt in judo."

And the physique to go with it, she thought. "It doesn't matter what they believe. Colton Reilly needs to think you had no part in my escape." Wrong word. Lily bit her lip.

"Too late."

He was right, of course, but her guilt was insurmountable. Lily lowered her voice. "The man's a killer. Until he's certain you won't serve as a lead to me, your life won't be worth two cents to him."

His frown deepened. "I'm no rookie."

"I know." She swallowed. "But I didn't understand how ruthless he was until two days ago. Now, because of me, you're in danger. That's hard to live with."

She met his gaze. His was icy, condemning. It said, *get to the point.*

"I might as well start with the worst part." Her stomach

flip-flopped and she took a deep breath. The stew she'd eaten was threatening to make a second appearance. "The social worker who transferred Annie's custody to me was murdered in our hotel. In my room."

He didn't even flinch. He'd been a good cop, she could tell. A hard one.

"Her name was Roberta Barker. After we signed the papers we went up to our rooms together. We switched because hers had double beds. I guess she called room service because when the porter came up he caught a man running out of her room. In fifteen minutes police were swarming the hotel."

He nodded. Lily knew he was committing the story to memory and would check every word that came out of her mouth. Until he did, she was a suspect. She took another deep breath. That was fair enough.

"Annie knew something bad was happening." She glanced at the bedroom door where the angelic child was sleeping. "She's...special."

A muscle in his jaw ticked, and something in his eyes changed.

"She woke me up and told me we had to leave. I didn't understand what was happening, and I panicked." She shrugged. "Actually, I still don't understand now."

His gaze fell to the table for only a second and then it was piercing hers again without mercy. She sighed and glanced around the room, not sure how to go on.

"Start by telling me your last name," he offered.

He truly was a good cop. At least he created the illusion he was making this easier for her.

"Brent. Lily Brent. My sister's name was Cassandra." And that seemed the best place to start. "When she was seventeen, she was struck by lightning."

Miles surprised her with a wry half-smile. He was strikingly handsome even through the severe lines he wore like a badge. She would bet when he smiled, *really* smiled, he was drop-dead gorgeous.

"And you're telling me this why?"

"She was convinced it gave her psychic powers." There, it was out. It made her sister sound crazy. Hell, it made *her* sound crazy.

"She was sitting under a pine tree with her boyfriend during a thunderstorm. He was killed. After that, Cassie changed. She withdrew from us and her friends. At first my mother and I believed she was reacting to her boyfriend's death, but then she tried to make us believe she could pick up other people's thoughts. She became obsessed with psychic phenomenon."

"What does this have to do with IntelliGenysis?"

She resisted another glance at the bedroom door. "My sister worked in the Telekinetic division."

His expression didn't change, but there was a barely perceptible raise of his brows. "I thought they did medical studies using gene therapy."

"They do. Cassie claimed IntelliGenysis was on the brink of developing a genetically superior future for mankind, building stronger, healthier, more intelligent babies through gene splicing. By identifying and isolating the genes which promote superior health, they also believe they have the potential to awaken undiscovered powers of the mind."

Lily read the disbelief in his face. "I know. It was hard for me to swallow too, especially considering Cassie's past behavior. Before she left for college, before she'd ever heard of Colton Reilly or IntelliGenysis, she was aggressively outspoken about the reality of psychic capabilities. She was almost obnoxious about it. But after she went to work there she changed. She was calm and professional and everything she said was described in scientific detail. It sounded plausible, if not frightening. I thought she'd found her niche. IntelliGenysis was a respected research facility intent on proving what she'd always believed in. She seemed happy, so I didn't question her."

"When was the last time you saw her?"

Lily stopped, thinking about the last nine years. For the first time since learning about her sister's death, tight sobs wound in the pit of her stomach. She took a deep breath, tamping them down. Crying would only look like a pitiful act to gain this suspicious man's sympathy.

"I'd only seen her twice since she left home. Cassie called me out of the blue about seven years ago. She needed a kidney transplant. I didn't think twice about it. She was my sister. Of course I would do it. She said she'd had a severe infection that damaged her kidneys. She was on dialysis and would die without a transplant. The procedure was done in the surgical center at IntelliGenysis."

His attention perked. "So you've been there, inside the compound?"

"After the surgery Colton Reilly tried to get me to take a job. I was offered more money than I'd ever dreamed of."

"You've met him personally?"

She nodded. "He's...calculating." It was the first word to come to mind that didn't sound nasty. Colton Reilly was arrogant and condescending. Beneath the golden-boy good looks most women found attractive, the man was oily, manipulative.

"I'm guessing you didn't take the job."

"It was suspicious from the start." And it only got worse,

but Lily kept the rest to herself. If she told him what she thought Colton really wanted her for, he would think she *was* crazy.

"I'm a graphic artist. I have no skills that would benefit them. The money and the chance to be closer to a family member would appeal to most people, but I built my company from the ground up. I'm sure you understand what it's like to own your own business. It's more than just a job. It's a part of me."

He shifted on his chair and leaned his elbows on the table, relaxing his defensive posture for the first time. He tipped his head. "Not the gas station," he admitted with another fleeting half-smile. "I used to feel that way about police work."

His grin vanished and his brows drew together, and like a wall, the harsh front was erected again.

Lily sighed. She wondered if he would let her see more of the real Miles before he handed her over to the Seattle PD. She experienced a momentary flicker of disappointment. This man was obviously nursing his own wounds, so wrapped up in his sorrow he didn't have time for her. But Lily was feeling lost and alone, and Miles Goodwin's chiseled good looks were as delicious as a cup of hot chocolate on a cold morning.

She glanced down at her hands on the table. Men who looked like Miles were out of her league. He thought she was a criminal. She could handle being looked at as plain and dull. She was used to that. But being a suspect was new to her, and Lily found it downright painful.

"Cassandra came home for Christmas four years ago, when our mother was still alive."

"What about your father?"

She shook her head. "He died a long time ago."

"Do you have any family left at all?" He made no effort to

soften the coldness of his question.

Lily laughed, but it was a pitiful, humorless sound. "I guess I don't. Just Annie." As she said it, a fierce welling of love surged inside her so powerfully it shook her. She would do anything for that little girl.

"Annie would have been about two, but Cassie never said a word about her. Our mother was living near me in an assisted-living community at the time. After we walked her home, Cassie started in about my working for IntelliGenysis again. She was so persistent I shouted at her to stop and told her not to bring it up again. She annoyed me so badly I was glad when she left."

This time Lily couldn't stop the tears burning her eyes. "That was the last time I saw her alive. Five days ago I got a call from the Spokane coroner's office, asking me to come and identify her body." She sat back, dropped her hands into her lap and stared at them.

Miles took a long breath in and out. "It must have been very difficult for you."

Shame burned in her gut as she shook her head. "I was more disappointed than sad, and now I feel guilty. We could have tried harder, she and I. But we didn't."

He didn't offer any condolences, and she was glad. She understood why he'd told her not to offer any earlier.

"And you learned about Annie then."

"Yes. Cassie's lawyer and the social services agent, Miss Barker, met me at the medical examiner's office and asked me to stay in town a day so we could take care of the paperwork right away. We checked in to the Country Home Suites at the same time. We signed papers that evening and were to process them at her office the next day."

"Why wasn't Annie given to her father?" Miles wore his suspicious, disbelieving face again.

"Colton Reilly wasn't married to my sister and his name isn't on the birth certificate. I'm not even certain he *is* Annie's father."

"Still—"

"My sister was run down in broad daylight while trying to escape from that man," she shot back. "Before she died she begged the hospital to make a video testament because she knew I would never believe her story unless she could tell me herself. They told her she was going to be all right but she knew she was going to die. She begged them until someone from the depositions office came in with a camera. Her video was a plea, begging me to take Annie away and keep her safe. At birth she'd legally named me as Annie's godparent, and if you saw the video you'd understand why the Department of Social Services didn't think twice about handing her over to me."

She was trembling and sweating and Miles had lost his doubting expression. But just when she was beginning to think he believed her, he asked, "Where is the video now?"

She sat back and crossed her arms over her chest, fighting to steady her shaking voice. "At your gas station."

Colton Reilly flipped open his cell phone when the ring identified Vince Luggo calling on the World Star satellite phone. "This better be good news."

"She got away from me."

Colton pinched the bridge of his nose. "How? She's a frightened woman headed home. You know where home is."

"She's using back roads. I caught up to her in Parkmont, but she tried to get away from me and crashed into a gas station."

"Dammit, I told you I didn't want her hurt."

"You said you wanted her scared. Trust me, she's scared."

"Where are you now?"

"Looking at the charred remains. She burned the place to the ground and took off with the attendant in a four-by-four. Thing is, I don't think he's your ordinary pump jockey."

"What do you mean?"

"I don't know. Something in the way he handled himself."

Colton bit back his irritation. "I don't want any witnesses."

"I'll take care of him."

"Be sure you tie up all loose ends, Vince. It's what I'm paying you for."

Vince snorted. "Don't worry, it'll be my pleasure."

"I'll have Quinlan track her by her cell phone. In the meantime, head to the police station. It's the most likely place they'll go."

Colton snapped the phone shut and buzzed his secretary. He handed her a slip of paper. "Tell Quinlan I have a job for him, and then find me whatever you can on the owner of this gas station and his employees."

She took the paper but remained in front of his desk. "Mr. Reilly, the Japanese are threatening to leave. They say if you don't meet with them in person by tomorrow morning, they're pulling out. They want their demonstration."

"Stall them another day."

"I've already stalled them two."

He took a calming breath. "I'll see them at nine tomorrow morning, but remind them they won't be able to see the demonstration until midnight. Have Dr. Shapiro prepare B2-8. We'll pull a switch and they'll never know the difference."

"Yes, sir."

"Get my information first."

He drummed his fingers as she strode back to her office. Even if Vince reclaimed A2-6 tonight, she wouldn't be ready to perform by tomorrow. She'd always been a strong-willed subject. This situation would make her unpredictable. She'd been out of her controlled environment for five days. It could take months to get her back under control and performing at her peak.

Three minutes later, Sandra buzzed his desk phone. "The sole proprietor is a Miles Goodwin, with no employees on record. He's ex-military on leave from Seattle PD. He was promoted to Investigations, but quit suddenly when his wife and daughter were killed in a car accident."

This was not good news. Lily Brent was in the care of a bleeding heart with special training and nothing to lose.

"Did they go to the local police?"

"Not so far as I can tell, but maybe they just haven't gotten there yet. He has a small house in Parkmont, a ski condo in Idaho and a beachfront cottage in Washington Bay. He must have invested well. He has almost no debt I can see."

Colton would bet money on the cottage. They were probably halfway to Seattle by now. It would be the most convenient place they could hole up near the cop's old stomping grounds.

"I'll need you to stay late tonight and monitor the police reports. Vince couldn't find his ass if his hands were cuffed behind his back."

Colton disconnected the call. Lily he could handle, but the cop was a problem.

He shook away his irritation. One inconvenience at a time.

As much as it goaded him to admit it, he needed the

Japanese. IntelliGenysis was doing well without foreign investors, but he wanted to move outside the strict regulations of the American drug industry. Recent breakthroughs demanded a new, updated facility, and he wanted Uncle Sam to see he wouldn't let the U.S. government take control. Opening a new facility in Canada would prove it. His groundbreaking achievements in genetics led the field. No other lab was even in the same race. Strategically placed spies kept him informed of that.

A2-6 was more successful than he'd dreamed possible. And Lily Brent—what a surprise she'd turned out to be. Cassandra had described her sister as meek, but she'd resisted his offers for employment twice, offers that were not meant to be refused. Now she defied him by fleeing even though she believed he would exert lethal force to get the child back.

Even more surprising was her courageous determination to protect a child she didn't even know. She had no idea how thick her blood ties truly were, but still she put the child's life first.

He was right in suspecting Lily was the key to A2-6's abilities.

Chapter Four

A strip of yellow light crossed the family room floor through the cracked bedroom door. After a few minutes of soft whispers, Lily and the child fell silent.

Miles picked up the Tigger doll. It was foolish to keep it away from the little girl like some coveted shred of his daughter. He'd donated her clothes and toys to a charity that helped women fleeing abusive relationships. This toy was no different, but his heart had seized with pain when he saw one last tangible piece of Michelle he could hold in his hand.

He rose from his chair and crossed the small family room. Miles gently pushed the door open.

Lily lay on her side, one arm placed over the sleeping child. Her molten gaze rose to his as he stepped into the room. Heat stirred in him, in of all places, his heart.

"You want me to turn out the light?"

She brushed a lock of corn silk hair from Annie's cheek and whispered, "She's afraid of the dark."

He'd already made the decision to dump these two at Seattle East's front door tomorrow morning and pretend he'd never met them. They couldn't be out of his world soon enough.

He looked down at the toy in his hand. Lily saw it too. There was pity in her eyes when she looked back into his. He crossed the room and placed it against Annie's arm. She would find it in the morning.

The gentle smile Lily thanked him with was more than he could bear. He turned and strode from the room.

He started by slipping into his shoulder holster. His feet took him to the wall safe behind Sara's small painting of the lake. His fingers turned the dial even as his mind warred with the hand wanting to hold the revolver again.

Turn them over to the department and forget you ever met them.

He knew that wasn't how it would happen. There was a part of the man he used to be, buried deep, that was still alive and wouldn't allow it.

Miles stayed up late into the night, taking great care cleaning his weapon. Hours later he was no closer to peace.

He loaded the cylinder and snapped it shut. The .38 fit his hand like a well-worn glove. It slipped naturally into his leather holster with the familiarity of a lover's kiss.

Of Lily's story, the part concerning him the most was the social worker's death.

Was a killer sleeping in the next room?

He tried to convince himself appearances could be deceiving. If the man who had chased her to the gas station had been a better shot, Lily would be the prime suspect in *his* murder.

He glanced at the short-wave radio on the credenza. Should he put a call in to local tonight? The clock beside it glowed eleven fifty-eight. At this time there would only be a desk officer on duty, but given the fire and the fact Miles couldn't be located, Sergeant Thompson might still be at the station.

Miles wiped his fingers on a rag and boxed up the gun-cleaning kit. A scraping sound behind him had him out of his chair and whirling toward the door. The .38 was in his hand before he'd made the decision to draw.

There was no one there. His eyes slipped to the picture that had lain face-down since the first—and last—time he'd come here after Sara's accident.

It was now standing up. His wife's smiling face taunted him over his own shoulder, her arms wrapped around his neck, her gleaming blond hair backlit by the late afternoon sun. In his arms Michelle smiled with all the youthful excitement of a playful child. His own face was that of a stranger he no longer recognized.

He turned away. Annie stood in the center of the tiny room.

"Sweetheart, you scared me."

Her eyes were wide, haunted. "I wanted to see them."

He turned back to the picture. He distinctly remembered glancing at it earlier, noting it was still laid down.

"Shouldn't you be in—"

Annie was gone.

An icy sensation rippled over his skin. Miles moved silently to the bedroom door and pushed it open. Annie and Lily lay in the same position they had been in hours earlier. Annie slept with one hand curled under her chin. Her brow was pinched and she twitched as though caught in a bad dream. Her little sneakers were beside the bedside table where her corduroy pants were folded neatly, exactly as they had been when he'd brought in the doll.

She'd been fully dressed as she stood in the cabin's main room, not thirty seconds ago.

He'd imagined it. He had to have. His senses were on overload and he needed sleep desperately. Coming out of his half-dead existence had been a shock to his system.

His body still hummed with nervous energy, but Miles went to the couch and lay down. He forced his eyes shut.

It seemed only moments later Lily shook him awake. Sunlight streamed in through the kitchen window. Recognition came rushing back with painful clarity.

Her beautiful face was a mask of terror. "Someone's coming."

Lily stood back as he bolted from the couch. Her frightened gaze widened when he drew the .38.

He went to the window over the sink and lifted the curtain. An engine surged and faded as a vehicle crested the hill on the dirt trail of his makeshift road and then slowed to cross the creek. He couldn't yet see the approaching vehicle, but he hoped the familiarity of the engine would prove true.

"It isn't the bad man." Annie stood in the doorway to the bedroom. He and Lily both glanced at her, but Lily was still tense.

A moment later, Eddie proved the little girl correct. Miles holstered the gun. "It's Edward Pierce. He was my sergeant before he retired. He's the friend I told you about; we share this cabin. His name is on the deed."

He stepped outside as Eddie pulled his Jeep Cherokee to a stop beside the porch. His old friend smiled and waved.

Miles went to the driver's door as Eddie shut off the engine. "You sure are a sight for sore eyes, pal. What the hell happened at the garage?"

"Small accident."

Eddie's worried gaze fell on Lily in the doorway and his brows crept up his forehead. "Well, that only adds to the confusion."

"Come on inside. I could use your advice."

Miles stepped back and noticed the boxes in the back of the Jeep. "You planning to stay a while? Looks like enough for an army."

"Never hurts to be prepared." Eddie waved his hand absently as he climbed out of the vehicle. "Local boys are looking for you. Them and the medical examiner. I sure am glad to find you in one piece."

"Eddie, this is Lily Brent." He gestured and Lily waved.

Eddie grinned. "Hello there, pretty lady."

Miles followed him to the back of the Jeep. Eddie opened the back and he and Miles each took a box. Lily came down and grabbed a third.

Eddie saw Annie when he stepped through cabin's doorway. "And who's this little angel?"

"This is my niece, Annie," Lily supplied. "Say hello, Annie."

She lingered shyly behind a kitchen chair. "'lo."

Eddie gave him a questioning glance as he began unloading supplies.

Lily moved past him into the kitchen and helped Eddie with the boxes. She held up a package of blueberries. "Ah, organics. A man after my own heart." She gave Eddie a smile that nearly melted Miles' heart.

"Lily, why don't you take Annie outside to play?" Miles made sure his tone left no room for argument. Lily's smile faded. She set down the blueberries and leveled a solemn gaze on him before calling to Annie.

"Say, I've got a baseball in the car," Eddie volunteered. "Why don't you two throw it around?"

Miles cringed. The old man always did have a better

bedside manner. He'd been a favorite public figure before he'd retired.

Eddie shoved two cartons of milk into the refrigerator and the four of them trailed outside. He retrieved the ball from the back of his Jeep and tossed it to Lily. She and the child moved into the open circle forming his dirt driveway.

Eddie settled beside him on the porch steps. He eased down slowly, and Miles could tell he tried to muffle the groan seeping out of him.

"You okay there, old man?" He said it jovially, but for the first time Miles noticed how quickly Eddie had aged in retirement.

"Nothing to worry about. I'm more concerned about you right now."

"I can only tell you what I know. Her car came barreling out of nowhere and crashed into my pumps."

"The police found two spent 9mm casings at the scene," Eddie said softly. "Is this woman holding you hostage?"

Miles laughed. "Come on, Ed."

"I can only tell you what I know," he threw back at Miles.

The light camaraderie brought back fond memories from his service years. Miles hadn't realized how much he missed this. How much he missed being a cop.

Lily tossed the ball to Annie. The little girl missed it and went scurrying after it, giggling with glee. Lily laughed and glanced over. Her smile turned into something that looked like bashfulness.

"She's awfully pretty," Eddie commented.

Miles shifted uncomfortably. He picked up a twig and tossed it off the porch. "Yeah."

Annie picked up the ball, awkwardly drew her arm back

and threw. She held on too long and the ball smacked the ground two feet in front of her.

Eddie laughed. "Gives new meaning to the term 'throwing like a girl'." He sighed. "The kid is cute, though."

"They're all cute." Miles refrained from adding, *but there's something strange about this one.*

"What's going on, Miles?"

"Someone chased them up the mountain using them for target practice. Her car was on its rims and out of control by the time it found my station. They got out alive, but whoever was after them tried to fix that. I've got a missing driver's side window and if the local boys look harder, they'll find a couple more casings."

"Jesus. Who would do that?"

Miles glanced at him. "A killer hired by Colton Reilly."

"That someone I'm supposed to know?"

"IntelliGenysis in Spokane."

Recognition and then anger filled Eddie's face. "That crackpot keeps popping up in the news like a turd that won't flush."

"He's the girl's father."

"I didn't know he was married."

"According to Lily, he wasn't. At least not to her sister." Miles pried an acorn from between two boards and flicked it away.

"Let me guess. The sister met a bad end."

Miles sighed. "I'm still trying to sort through all that."

Eddie shook his head. "You really stuck your foot in it this time."

"I'm taking them to Seattle and turning them over to

Billings. Then I'm out of it." He wondered if he should tell Eddie about the social worker. The old man looked so tired he didn't want to add any strain.

"You going to be able to drop them there and walk away?"

Miles watched Annie try to throw again. It would seem she had never held a ball before, let alone tried to throw one. But she was having a good time, laughing and running and giving her best effort, and that was good for her.

"I don't know." He wasn't lying to Eddie. Somehow, without his consent, a protective urge had crept under his skin and fixed itself against his heart. Lily tried to keep a courageous front, but he saw the desperation in her frightened eyes every time she looked at him. It didn't matter she was beautiful and alone. Dead soul or not, on the payroll or not, he would never turn his back on a person in mortal danger.

But neither could he lie to himself. He was painfully aware of those melted-chocolate eyes, the slight curve of her small nose, the soft lines of a face pretty enough to grace the cover of a fashion magazine. She was nearly as tall as he was, with a narrow waist that flared into womanly hips and long legs that went all the way to town.

He dragged his gaze away. "I need your Jeep. It won't be safe for us in my truck."

"It's yours," Eddie assured him.

"Whoever tried to plug her saw my truck. I'll leave you the keys so you can get out if you need to, but no touring."

"I don't plan to go anywhere," Eddie said over another sigh. He looked over and found Miles' assessing gaze.

"What's really going on with you, Pops?" Miles used the familiar nickname to let his old friend know he had no intention of letting him out of an explanation.

Eddie tore a frayed strand off the bottom of his Levis. Annie drew back her arm to throw, lost her grip on the ball and sent it straight up into the air. Eddie laughed, but his expression sobered quickly.

"The big C."

"Jesus, Ed. I didn't know."

"I didn't let you know. First time was four years ago. I had colon cancer but I beat it. I was free and clean for two years, and then they found it in my lung. You thought I was on a fishing trip in Alaska."

"You old dog. Why didn't you tell me?"

"You had your own problems by then."

Miles felt like a dirt bag. He'd been destroyed by grief and had let the rest of his life slip. There'd been no room for socializing, no room for another woman, no room for living. But he loved Eddie like a father, and he'd been too blinded by his own pain to see his friend's.

"I'm sorry."

"Nothing to be sorry about. This is God's plan."

"I wish I'd been there for you. You shouldn't go through this alone."

"Oh, *pshaw*. Just because you didn't know doesn't mean I was alone." He turned and gave Miles a piercing stare. "Listen to me, youngster."

Eddie had assigned the moniker to all the young cops. Miles gave a chuckle at the nickname he'd nearly forgotten while inside he felt the last solid pieces of his world crumbling away.

"I know you've had a hard time finding reason these past few years, but take it from someone who knows, mortality is a lot less comforting when you're staring it in the face."

It was official. He was pond scum.

"I miss Claire something awful, but I'm in no hurry to join her."

"I would trade places with you if I could. I owe you my life, several times over. The Christy Street bust, Ricardo Mendez. Probably a few I'm forgetting about."

"Thank God it's not up to you. Everything happens for a reason, Miles. Don't you forget that."

Eddie was right. Miles never counted much on divine intervention, the stars or destiny determining the preconceived route of men's lives, but something had brought Lily and Annie to him.

He looked over and caught Lily's curious gaze. She offered another shy smile before reaching to catch Annie's throw. The part of him that wanted to help her was growing bigger, like a withering house plant that had been watered and placed out in the sun. He wasn't even sure it was an unwelcome thing anymore.

And that scared the hell out of him.

Chapter Five

Miles' friend pushed off the step. "Here honey, let me give you a few pointers." He ambled over to Annie and knelt behind her. "Hold the ball in your hand like this. Yep, that's right. Now, when you throw it let it slip through your fingers." With Eddie's help the ball soared toward Lily.

Miles stood and strode over to her. "Take a walk with me."

Whatever shreds of comfort she'd felt tossing the ball back and forth vanished in an instant. Mr. Cop was back, and probably ready to read her the riot act. She could only assume with another seasoned cop's advice, Miles was feeling less generous toward her. She'd seen them talking, it didn't take subtitles to know what they'd been saying. *Give her to the cops. This isn't your problem.*

She glanced at Annie.

"She'll be fine."

He took her by the arm and steered her away, no arguments allowed. In the next instant, he jerked his hand away as if her skin had burned him.

The poor man was so despondent over his wife's death he couldn't even touch her. She wondered what it would be like to know that kind of love. A strange mixture of jealousy and remorse hit the pit of her stomach. However short their marriage, Miles' wife had been a lucky woman.

Lily looked over her shoulder. Edward tossed the ball gently to Annie, who managed to catch it. She smiled as Annie squealed with delight.

Miles stopped under a massive pine and leaned back, one foot propped against its trunk. "I want you to know I'm not going to abandon you in Seattle. Things might get a little intense, but I'll be right there with you."

Meaning, *you'll be interrogated and I'm going to take part.*

"Thank you," she said automatically.

"You said you'd been inside IntelliGenysis. What can you tell me about the compound?"

"It was seven years ago. That's what I can tell you."

He met her gaze steadily and Lily let herself drink in those deep blue eyes. They'd grown lighter in the morning sun, as still and clear as Caribbean waters.

"You might as well tell me what you can."

"Why, so you can identify discrepancies in my story when I'm questioned?"

He seemed taken aback she'd recognized the tactic.

"I heard you last night," she threw at him. "You asked Annie if I kidnapped her."

Miles' expression hardened. "Do you blame me?"

Her shoulders sagged and what little energy she had waned. He was trying to help in the only way he knew how: by the book.

"I'm sorry. I didn't sleep well." She stopped before telling him bad dreams and a pounding headache had driven her to the bathroom to throw up, and that was when she heard the approaching Jeep. "I wouldn't expect any less of you. I wouldn't want any less for Annie."

"Look, I don't suspect you of wrongdoing. But I have to ask, what did you think you were going to do?"

She shrugged. "I truly don't know. I called my lawyer and told him I would need help with a custody issue." She drew a shaky breath. "Since then this has soared out of his league."

"You were just going to run home and close the curtains?"

His tone was hard and Lily felt like a fool—both for being so stupid and for daydreaming about him. Miles was an official who saw her as a suspect. He probably hated her for involving him in her problems.

"Something like that. I told you, he didn't actually shoot at me until last night."

Miles shoved his hands in the front pockets of jeans clinging snugly to distinct thigh muscles. With a plaid cotton shirt rolled up to the elbows, he looked like the sexy man on the Brawny paper towel labels. His suspicious stance relaxed a notch, but Lily could tell he was still uneasy about the whole situation.

She couldn't blame him. When he'd first said he used to be a cop, warning chimes had gone off in her head. Now she realized what a stroke of luck it was landing in the hands of someone with police training.

"I really appreciate everything you're doing for me. I know it isn't easy for you," she said, feeling bad for being curt with him.

He glanced away and didn't seem to be listening. It made Lily feel even more like an inconvenience.

"I'll try to intrude on your life as little as possible."

Miles took a step in the direction of the cabin. Edward and Annie were sitting on the porch steps.

"Eddie?"

The older man was bent forward, holding Annie's hands like an anchor to keep from falling over. Miles broke into a run and Lily hurried after him.

Edward was shaking. Sweat beaded on skin that had turned gray.

"Eddie, what's wrong?"

He let out a shuddering breath. It appeared to Lily he was having a heart attack.

Miles reached for Annie. "Come here, sweetheart."

"No!" Eddie barked through clenched teeth. "Leave her alone."

Miles stood back and brushed against her, and Lily brought her hand up to his shoulder, steadying him. He slipped his arm around her too, and though Lily knew he wouldn't have done it if he wasn't distracted, she let herself take comfort nonetheless. His hand at the small of her back felt strong and reassuring.

"Give me your keys. I'll go for a doctor."

"No need. I'm all right." Some of Edward's color was coming back and his breathing returned to normal. "I just... I'm all right now."

Annie leaned against his shoulder and put her arm around his neck. She smiled at them as though nothing were wrong.

"Did you have an episode?" Miles asked him.

Edward looked at him. "Yes. An episode. We were talking about baseball and I got dizzy. Isn't that right, Annie?"

She nodded. "Can we throw the ball some more?"

"How about we go inside and eat breakfast instead?" Eddie asked her. He managed a smile. "I brought milk but it'll go bad before I can drink it all."

Miles moved away, leaving a void of cold air rushing across Lily's body. He took Eddie by the hand and helped him to his feet. He clapped him on the back, revealing a friendship that
54

went much deeper than two old coworkers crossing paths. "Come on, old man. No more episodes, all right?"

Was this another strange incident with Annie? Lily chewed a fingernail. Had the child done something to harm him?

"What do you mean, *episode?*" she whispered as Eddie went inside in front of them. "Is he asthmatic?"

Miles scowled and shook his head. She took it as a clear message not to ask questions.

Annie hopped into a kitchen chair while Eddie went into the narrow kitchen. "What do you want, kiddo? Strawberry-O's or wheat crisps?" He took two cereal boxes out of a paper bag and set them on the counter dividing the kitchen from the small cabin's great room.

"Mmm...strawberry."

"Let me," Miles said.

"Nonsense," Eddie argued. "I'm fine. Just a little nauseated. The radiation does it to me. Don't worry, it passed."

Lily sat across from Annie. She stayed silent as she battled with an odd mixture of relief and sadness. She looked at the older man with new eyes and new sympathy for Miles. Radiation meant cancer. Miles could lose another person close to him.

"I'm going to take a shower," Miles said. "Then I'm going to head into town to the station. I want to see if any of your belongings survived the fire. We'll head out for Seattle as soon as I get back. Be ready to go."

That either meant *with me* or *in cuffs*. Lily bit her tongue before asking him if he'd like a fingerprint to take with him.

"What about you, little lady. What would you like?" Edward beamed at her. He didn't appear to hold her under the suspicion Miles did, but then again, she hadn't burned his gas station to the ground. And whatever had been wrong with him a few minutes ago, he seemed to have recovered quickly.

"Strawberry-O's will be fine, thank you." She wouldn't ask Edward to open a second box of cereal just for her. She could tolerate an artificially flavored cereal once. Beggars couldn't be choosers, and Colton Reilly had reduced her to a helpless, vulnerable tramp.

Her stomach still churned from the turbulent dreams of the night before and tears were dangerously close. Combined with Miles' standoffish disinterest, her mood was fragile.

Miles emerged from the shower in record time. His hair was tousled and damp, softening his chiseled appearance. He stepped into the great room in a soft blue shirt with the buttons undone. The pale color made his eyes look like sapphires. His chest was hairless, and remnants of a tan on a washboard stomach ended just above the waistline of faded Levi's.

Eddie tossed him a ring of keys. Miles reached high to grab them and his shirt opened further, displaying a sexy weave of muscle over bone.

Lily looked away quickly. A Strawberry-O lodged in her throat.

"You know where the key is?" he asked Edward with a glance to the far corner of the room.

"Of course," the older man replied solemnly. Lily understood they were talking about the rifle case.

Miles left without another word.

"Hey there, kiddo, how about some more cereal?" He sat beside Annie.

"Thank you."

The old man looked at Lily. In his eyes she found kindness. "He's a little rough around the edges, but he's had a hard time."

She nodded.

"So have you, I gather."

She bit out a laugh. "You don't know the half of it."

But she was still alive, and Lily counted herself lucky. Miles' wife and child were gone, and Edward was staring the grim reaper in the face. She knew enough to count her blessings.

"You worked with Miles on the police force?"

"I was his sergeant for three years before I retired. He was a hot-headed rookie when he first came aboard."

She smiled. "I can picture that." She imagined him in official dress with a shining silver badge. His eyes must have been downright magical against the dark blue uniform.

"It's a damn shame at thirty-four he thinks his life is over." Edward sighed and rose from the table. "I'll make you some sandwiches for the road. What's your fancy, little one? Peanut butter or jelly. No, wait—I've got it. How about both?"

Annie giggled and Lily managed a smile while her thoughts lingered on the bereft man who had left here.

When Miles smiled he looked younger. She guessed if he smiled more often it might become easier. She wished he would, not just because she would love to see how utterly handsome it would make him, but because she wished he *felt* more like smiling.

"He lost his wife and daughter?"

Edward nodded. "They were killed by a drunk driver. Miles had personally arrested the man once before, but the guy was a politician with a lot of influence. Hardly made a dent in his drinking career."

"How terrible for him."

"Miles and Sara were close. She'd had trouble conceiving.

57

Michelle was their miracle child. She meant the world to them."

Lily looked away as a lump formed in her throat. Why did the most tragic events happen to the happiest families? She could tell that beneath his hard exterior Miles was an honorable man with a noble character who would do anything for the people he loved.

Would she ever find that kind of love?

She found herself under Annie's curious gaze.

"Are they in heaven too?"

"Yes honey, they are. But it makes Mr. Miles really sad so we shouldn't ask him about them."

"They miss him too."

She glanced at Edward. He didn't seem to find her statement strange.

"Of course they do," he said, busily making sandwiches. "But heaven is a good place where all souls are safe."

"Are we gonna go there some day?"

"Not for a very long time," Lily assured her.

"He said there is no such thing as heaven, but my mommy said he was wrong."

"Who did, Annie?" Edward asked her.

"The man." She spooned another mouthful of strawberry cereal. "This tastes good. How come I can't see the strawberries?"

Lily chuckled. "Because they're very small."

"What man?" Edward pressed.

"Mr. Reilly. He's my daddy but he doesn't let us call him that."

Edward's gaze pierced her. "Us?"

"I have nineteen brothers and sisters."

Annie's spoon slipped into the bowl and milk spattered. She seemed more concerned with wiping it off her hand than the gaping stare Lily returned.

"I know he's wrong, though," Annie continued innocently. "Heaven is real. I know people who live there."

Chapter Six

On his way down the mountain, Miles passed the gas station. Yellow barrier tape roped off the pumps but the building appeared unaffected.

"Another couple of years and those pumps would have been antiques," he said aloud. Not that he would have been around for it. Historical building or not, the garage was a depressing pit.

The whole town was a heartbreaking reminder of his family. But leaving Parkmont would mean leaving Sara and Michelle. They were buried here in the Harris family plot.

His in-laws would be glad the station was destroyed. Montgomery Harris had petitioned the city to have the place torn down. He'd cited it as an eyesore tarnishing Parkmont's character and depreciating land values. The city had refused. The station had been built in nineteen twenty-two and with its gas pumps from nineteen sixty-two, it was officially a historic landmark.

Miles put his foot back on the gas and brought Eddie's Cherokee up to speed. Not for the first time since leaving the cabin did he question his involvement with Lily Brent. He should just cart her to Seattle and dump her on Billings. Getting involved would only get him hurt. *Or killed.*

Guilt niggled at the back of his mind. Caring about them

was almost a betrayal to his family's memory. He tried to convince himself his odd and sudden attraction to Lily was just old-fashioned lust. She was an exceptionally beautiful woman, and he was still a man. After three years of solitude, his body was aching for release.

He could live without it, he told himself. And Lily didn't strike him as the kind of loose woman who would sympathize with his sexual frustration and toss him a pity fuck.

But the part of him that was still a cop had to know if her story checked out. The little girl deserved as much.

Miles angled the Cherokee into the small police station's visitor lot and shut off the engine. Despite his gut instinct telling him Lily was innocent of any serious wrongdoing, he still felt an uncomfortable tremor of suspicion where she was concerned, and he half-expected to find Annie's face on a missing child poster in the station's vestibule as he walked through the doors.

"Well, isn't that a fine how do you please?" Sergeant Noah Thompson bellowed from the doorway of his office. Behind him Joe Howell, the fire chief, sat in an old-fashioned drafter's chair. "We spend half the night looking for you, expecting to find little pieces of you stuck to the trees, and you walk in here as happy as ever."

"Happy isn't part of the equation," Miles said with a grin. He walked over and shook the man's hand. "How you doing, Noah?"

"That's the question I want you to answer. Chief Howell put out a two alarm at your station last night."

"Shame about the pumps, isn't it? I thought they might be worth some money some day."

"Why'd you leave the scene?" Noah ignored Miles' jovial front. "You of all people should know better."

Miles ground his teeth as he tried to keep a casual expression. "My truck was behind the garage so I thought it safest to stay away from the fire. The woman and I exchanged insurance information and I took her to the rental car agency through the valley."

"You didn't call anyone."

"My cell didn't have reception."

Noah crossed his arms. "We found casings from a 9mm near the highway."

"Mine. I chased off a cougar the other night."

The police chief frowned. Miles knew ballistics would prove him wrong soon enough. Thank goodness things worked slowly in a small town.

"I told her I would collect her stuff and see if the car was salvageable."

At this Noah snorted. "The car is toast." His scowl deepened. "If you were anyone else, you know what I'd say."

"But I'm not anyone else. I'm the man who always lets you claim you hauled in the bigger fish."

Noah barked out a laugh. "Yeah, right." He turned and called to one of his deputies. "Get the woman's purse and suitcase."

Miles breathed a sigh of relief. Had they not been friends and Miles an ex-cop, her belongings would have been locked up in evidence until she showed up and explained what had happened—probably with a lawyer standing next to her.

"I know if she'd been drinking you'd have slapped the cuffs on her yourself." Noah raised his eyebrows, confirming his suspicion the chief's leniency with him was part pity.

Miles bit back his comments.

"But this close to the holidays I want a clean plate. If you're not pressing charges, that's good enough for me."

He shrugged. "Nothing to press charges for."

The deputy emerged with a charred purse that had once been a light cream color and a small suitcase in even worse condition. He dropped the purse on the sergeant's desk. It smelled like melted plastic and burnt leather.

Miles opened Lily's wallet. Her driver's license proved she had not lied about her name. It eased his suspicions a centimeter. He slipped an insurance card out of her wallet and held it up for Thomson to see. "She's fully insured, and so am I." He mustered a grin. "Looks like Montgomery Harris gets his wish. I'm not rebuilding. A Master Craft Deep Sea sounds a lot more appealing right about now."

"Gonna take the money and run, are you?" Sergeant Thompson laughed along with him. "Can't say as I blame you."

Miles found the video tape. Though the inside of Lily's purse was undamaged, the video might have been melted by the heat. He hoped it would still work. "Mind if I use an interrogation room?" He held up the small cassette. It would need a special adapter to be played in a standard VCR.

Noah was still skeptical. The older man's eyebrows crawled up his face like twin caterpillars. "Mind if I watch it with you?"

"No problem." A prickling of unease danced across his skin. But if the video somehow incriminated Lily, so be it.

They went to an interrogation room where a television and video player sat on an AV cart. Noah fitted the eight millimeter tape into an adapter cassette and slid it into the player. After a few minutes of static, the screen filled with the somewhat shaky, hand-held image of a hospital emergency room.

A woman with dirty blond hair lay on a hospital bed surrounded by frantic medical personnel. The hair was matted flat against her head with blood on one side. Two nurses were cutting off her blood-spattered shirt. She was pale and in obvious pain.

"Okay, go ahead ma'am," a voice said off camera.

The blond woman looked at the camera and winced. She pulled an oxygen mask away from her mouth and Miles heard her seize a sharp breath before starting. "Lily, Lily, I'm so sorry." Her voice was strained as she struggled to speak. "I've made a mess of my life, and Annie's too."

A doctor with graying hair entered the scene. The nurses eased her onto her side so the man could work on her back. The woman on the bed craned toward the camera and the videographer came around the side of the bed, only to be jostled by a nurse who shot a dirty look at the camera.

The woman cried out in pain.

"It's okay, Cassandra. I just want to see what I'm up against. Nurse, get me a sponge." There was a flash of gore as the doctor pulled back a flap of skin to look inside the wound. Miles' stomach lurched.

Cassandra's face contorted and she screamed in pain. A nurse bent over her, blocking the view. The camera operator shifted to the right in time to catch two tears rolling over pale cheeks.

"I've left IGS. It was no place to raise a child. It's horrible there, Annie hated it. Colton treated her like a lab rat. Please, take her someplace safe." She gasped in pain. "My lawyer, Doug Ross at Ross and White...he has my will and the key to my safety-deposit box."

"We need to get you into X-ray, Cassandra. Your ankle is broken and I suspect a few ribs as well."

"Really?" Cassandra snapped. "You went to medical school for that? It's bent backward, for God's sake. Ouch! Jesus, be careful!"

"We'll get you something for the pain right away. Lean over for me, please. You've got a nasty compound back here."

"I've been waiting here almost forty minutes. You can wait two." She craned toward the camera. "Lily, I know I have no right to ask anything of you, but I'm not asking for me, I'm asking for Annie. Please, she needs you. You're her..." The woman's voice faded over a gurgle.

"I've dislodged a clot. We've got a bleeder here, hemostat."

As though she felt her life slipping away, Lily's sister reached desperately toward the camera.

"You're all she's got. I named you as her godmother when she was born. I'm sorry I didn't tell you about her...but now I need you to put aside...forgive me."

Some of her words were drowned out by the escalating chaos in the room.

"Page the OR," the doctor shouted. "Get the surgeon down here, *now!* Open those fluids up."

"I know I can trust you. You'll know what to do. You've always been the mature one. Please don't let me down." Her voice faded and she sagged onto the bed. "Please, Lily. Please. Take her somewhere...safe."

"Heart rate one sixty-two. BP's falling."

A machine beeped out a warning. A nurse moved the oxygen mask back into place. Cassandra's eyes rolled back in her head and her lids fluttered closed.

"V-FIB. Start CPR, bag her, give me two units O neg and shock her at three-sixty."

Cassandra was rolled onto her back. One of the doctors began CPR while a nurse pulled the mask away and used a balloon to start her breathing again. The doctor readied the paddles. They charged up with an ominous whine.

"Let's go people. Clear!"

Cassandra's body arched off the bed. The heart rate monitor registered two irregular beats and then went flat.

The nurse who'd given the dirty look turned to the camera. She held up a hand in front of the lens. "Out." A blurred shot of the floor swept across the screen. The video went black.

A long moment of hollow silence bounced off the walls of the interrogation room.

"Sweet Jesus," Noah finally said.

Miles was sweating. The video brought back horrific memories of a night spent in an antiseptic-scented emergency room while doctors rushed desperately to save Michelle. In the end, the silence that fell had been like lead in his ears.

He felt the same way now. Bile rose in his throat and Miles was grateful he hadn't eaten anything this morning.

Lily's story was true on all accounts, but it was no easier to accept.

Noah rose and shut off the television. His voice cut through the heavy silence. "You want to tell me what's really going on?"

I wish I knew, Miles thought. "The 'Colton' she referred to is Colton Reilly."

"Ah. And does Colton Reilly own a 9mm semi-automatic?"

Miles rose and ejected the tape. He removed the cassette from the video adapter and slipped it into his pocket.

"Miles, I can help you."

"You already have."

"Don't try to do this alone."

"I'm not doing anything but giving her back her stuff. I'm going to let Will Shapiro handle the insurance matter."

Noah frowned. "Don't be a maverick."

Clearly the sergeant didn't believe him. That was okay. It was still better if he didn't know the whole story. "It's nice to know I can depend on you." He nodded toward the blank screen. "She lives in Seattle, so I think it would be better if I called Billings."

"Hmm."

"You know it's nothing personal. Look, you've been a good friend over the years, especially when..." Miles clenched his jaw and glanced away. "I'd feel better if you weren't involved. You said you wanted a clean plate."

Noah only nodded over an exasperated sigh. "Whatever your reasons, I'm not here to judge. Officially I gotta tell you to go by the book. But unofficially, you know I look out for my own, even if you weren't mine but one of them snooty, big city cops."

Miles chuckled.

"You call me—off the record—if you need me."

"Thanks, Noah."

Still frowning, he shook his head. "I shouldn't let you walk out of here." He cuffed Miles on the shoulder as he followed him out of the interrogation room. "Just don't make me sorry I did."

Miles gnashed his teeth as he drove back up the mountain. His mood had turned foul.

He didn't like knowing Lily had told the truth. He didn't want to look into those soft, brown eyes and believe their desperation. Didn't want to know she was innocent and helpless.

It would be easier to resist her if she was a criminal. Easier, but not effortless.

The fact she was risking her life to save a child she hardly knew, the daughter of the sister she hardly knew, thawed shards of ice off his frozen heart.

She'd tried to hijack his truck with a rusted antenna. It was almost cute. Definitely pathetic. He couldn't believe she'd gotten this far with a diabolical mastermind hot on her heels.

He arrived back at the cabin to find Eddie and Annie tossing the ball back and forth. Edward looked expectantly in his direction, having recognized the approaching sound of his own vehicle.

"I guess she checked out." He gave a knowing smile and tossed the ball gently back to Annie, who managed to catch it this time.

Miles nodded while inside his head he grumbled. Leave it to Eddie to be right all the time.

He found Lily inside tidying the kitchen. She stopped mid-swipe across the countertop, looking like a mouse that realized it had crept in front of a cat.

Miles stepped into the mouth of the narrow kitchen. He waited until she set down the washrag and faced him. Her eyes were wide, but a little sad. None of this had been easy for her, but he'd been thinking only about himself. He guessed he owed her an apology.

Her gaze flicked to the blackened purse in his hand. He set it on the counter.

"Your story checks out."

"I know."

She met his eyes, but her expression didn't change. He'd forgotten how sensitive women could be. She hadn't liked being doubted. He would give that apology if he could only muster the words.

"I wouldn't be doing my job right if I simply took your word for everything." That was as close as he could come.

She snatched her purse and opened it. Her shoulders relaxed when she saw the cassette in the center compartment.

"Are you a cop again?"

"I never stopped being one."

A tremor of a smile flickered at the corners of her mouth.

"Did you watch it?"

He nodded. "I'm sorry I had to intrude on your privacy."

"It's all right." She zipped the purse shut. "I'm just thankful it wasn't damaged. Child Protective Services has a copy, but I feel better having one too. It's my only weapon to fight him."

Lily turned around and rinsed out the dishcloth she'd been using to wipe the counters. He stood there, numb, as she dried the utensils she'd hand washed and dropped them back in the drawer. Still the apology wouldn't come. To say it would be to offer a tender emotion to her, and Miles wasn't up to that yet. He might never be.

"Edward said we could borrow his Jeep," she said softly, as though she felt his emotions and was sympathetic to them. Yep, he'd definitely forgotten how sensitive women could be.

"You don't have to come with us. I live close to Seattle East Station. I know how to get there on my own."

"Do you think you can make it without me?"

"I know how to drive." She managed another timid smile. It cut into Miles like a knife. "Though you will have to take my word on that."

Miles glanced away before her sweet smile caught him by the throat. He swallowed. "You need me. And I wouldn't feel right letting you go alone."

When he met her eyes again, her smile was gone.

"You're right, Miles. I do need you." A trembling frown pinched between her brows. "I'm so scared I can hardly draw a breath. But I know you don't want to be with us, and I respect that."

She broke then, and his frozen heart disintegrated into a thousand sharp shards. Lily covered her face with her hands and sobbed. He jerked, instinctively moving to take her in his arms. But his spine stiffened and his body went numb, preventing him from taking the step that would bring them together.

Lily leaned back against the counter. She sniffled and wiped at the tears on her cheeks with the back of her hand. "Sorry."

"Don't be. If you didn't cry I would think there was something wrong with you."

"My life changed in a single day. The phone rang, I picked it up and suddenly I was on a different course."

Miles stepped closer and lifted his hand to touch her shoulder. At the last minute he thought better of it. "I know all about how that feels."

There was nothing more catastrophic than learning someone had died. He'd searched through his disintegrating sanity for a way to fix it, but there was none. It left him feeling broken and useless, like a machine gnashing over a broken gear.

"Things had been good for me. I'd worked hard for that. Now I don't know what to do. If they can't prove he killed my sister and put him away forever, I'll never be safe."

"There are good men in Seattle who can help you. I'll make sure you find them. You'll be safe. You and Annie both."

Lily drew a deep breath and surprised him by smiling. "They say when you have a child you develop an instant sense of self-sacrifice. That the child becomes more important to you than your own life. In a way, that happened to me. I adored Annie the very instant I laid eyes on her. I would do anything to keep her safe."

"I don't even know her and I feel that way," he said. It was true—it just killed him that she reminded him of Michelle.

"I'll bet you feel that way about all kids."

"Most cops do."

"I never did." She laughed, but it was a choked sound. "I didn't even particularly like kids."

Lily leaned away from the counter and straightened her shoulders. "I'm sorry to lay all that on you." She touched his arm. Strangely, this time it didn't hurt the pit of his stomach.

"I meant what I said. I don't want you to feel obligated. Seattle is only four hours away, and nobody will recognize us in Edward's Jeep. I'm sure we can make it to the police station by ourselves."

Her fingers drew away, leaving a little trail of tingles behind.

"And I meant what I said. I wouldn't be able to live with myself if I let you go alone."

Annie burst through the door and Eddie followed behind.

"Hi, Mr. Miles."

"Hi, Annie. Are you ready to go?"

"Uh huh." She held up the baseball. "Mr. Eddie said I could keep the ball. He says I need more practice."

"Did you say thank you?" Lily asked. She gave a subtle swipe at a stray tear and disguised her misery well.

"She sure did," Eddie said, winking.

Miles stepped closer to his old friend. "How are you doing?"

"Ten times better than I was yesterday," Eddie assured him.

Miles would have thought Eddie was mollifying him if the old man didn't look so much better. He stepped back and clapped his hands together. "Okay, if you have to pee, do it now."

Annie's eyes grew wide and her mouth formed a perfect circle. Her pale cheeks burned red as she turned and ran for the bedroom.

"She's a doll," Eddie told Lily. "You're very lucky."

Miles would swear the same blush crept into Lily's cheeks.

"I know."

They loaded up and Miles watched Annie buckle her seatbelt in the rearview mirror. He rolled down the window as Eddie came alongside.

"I'll be back by noon tomorrow."

"Do what you gotta do. Don't worry about the heap." Eddie tapped the doorframe twice and stepped back. "God be with you."

Eddie stood on the porch as the Jeep's engine faded. Soon there was nothing but the sound of the Washington wilderness rushing through the tops of ancient Ponderosa pine. He stepped onto the rich earth and breathed deeply.

He stretched his arms out to the sides, flexing the muscles in his back. The section under his left arm where lymph nodes had been removed in four different surgeries no longer hurt. His lower back, where biopsy needles had been inserted into his liver and kidneys more times than he could count, no longer hurt.

For the first time in two years, he could draw a deep breath without the tight, constricting feeling in the right side of his chest where half his lung had been removed.

The weakness was gone. The ache, the nausea, the heavy feeling as though lead ran through his veins.

All of it gone.

He took another deep breath, reveling in the miracle that had occurred. Tears filled his eyes.

He looked to the sky and gave silent thanks to God for sending Annie to him. He didn't know what he'd done to deserve this gift, but he knew one thing for sure, his cancer was gone.

Chapter Seven

Annie squealed with delight as the Jeep bounced over the forest floor.

"I like this better than driving on the road."

Miles grinned. Annie's laughter was contagious. "My kinda' girl."

Lily felt Miles glance at her, but she was afraid to take her eyes off the track in front of them. She sat stiffly in the seat and gripped the assist handle.

"We're almost to the highway," he told her.

Out of nowhere they were overtaken by a herd of deer. At least twenty, some with enormous antlers, came upon them from the right and galloped along with the Jeep.

"Watch out!" Lily shrieked. One of the larger animals cut in front of the vehicle.

Miles had already taken his foot off the gas; now he stomped on the brake.

"What are they?" Annie asked.

"They're deer." But unlike any deer Lily had ever seen. How odd they would charge up to a moving vehicle like this.

"You've never seen a deer before?" Miles asked Annie. He glanced into the rear view mirror.

"Uh-uh."

The animals came to a complete stop and surrounded the Jeep, snorting out plumes of frosty breath into the brisk air. It was downright eerie. Their obsidian eyes looked straight into the Jeep as though searching for something.

"Are they dangerous?" Lily whispered. "What would make them do this?"

Suddenly, as one, they spooked and sprang away, vanishing into the trees as quickly as they had appeared.

"We must have surprised them. If one runs they all head in the same direction. Fight or flight theory, I guess." He started the Jeep forward again.

She glanced at him. Miles didn't seem suspicious that Annie might have had something to do with the bizarre incident. He was probably thinking about how strange it was she had lived her whole life in Washington without ever seeing a deer.

He slowed the Jeep to a crawl as they dipped through a gully beside the highway and climbed onto the pavement. "It was strange, though," he said softly. "I've never seen anything like that."

"They were beautiful. I'd hate to see one of them get run over by a four wheeler." As the track smoothed out Lily craned around to see into the back seat and smiled at Annie. "I like the road better."

Annie laughed. "That was fun. Can we do it again?"

"Sure we can," Miles told her with another glance into the mirror.

Lily bit her lip. She didn't know much about children, but promising things he couldn't deliver definitely seemed wrong.

The next two hours were spent in a stiff silence broken only by Annie's many questions. From the corner of her eye, Lily saw

Miles clench his jaw several times. Annie's cheerful chatter probably reminded him of road trips with his daughter, but Lily couldn't think of a way to make her stop short of suggesting she take a nap.

They passed several roadside rest stops maintained by the national forestry service. The closer they got to Seattle, the fewer and farther between they became.

"Are you getting hungry, pumpkin?"

Annie nodded and perked up, peering out of the window. "Can we stop for a while?"

"The next time you see one of those public rest areas would you mind stopping?" she asked Miles. The closer to home they got the higher Lily's spirits rose, but she needed to use the restroom and knew she'd never make it all the way to the police station.

Miles pulled over at a rest stop sixty-five miles from the city limits. Steel gray clouds filled the sky, squeezing out narrow rays of sun trying to reach the earth. Despite the darkening sky, they followed a wooded path to an area with picnic tables below the line of sight of the highway and ate the sandwiches Edward had prepared.

Another car stopped near the restrooms. Annie watched two kids run past, down a short slope to a play area.

"What is that?" she asked when the little boy swung from the monkey bars.

Lily glanced up into Miles' questioning eyes. "It's a jungle gym."

His suspicious gaze flicked to Annie. "When you lived with your mommy, did you ever play outside?" He softened his frown almost as if he had to remind himself to, and the resulting smile looked contrived.

Annie nodded shyly. "We did special stuff."

"Like what?"

Across the picnic area, the parents called to their kids, who bolted back up the hill to the parking lot.

"Um, calisthenics." Annie watched them, fascinated. She threw a pointed look at Lily. "Can I go to the jungle gym?"

"Once we finish our sandwiches we'll all go over," Lily promised. She might even take a swing on the bars herself. She needed to stretch her road-weary muscles and a little exercise would help clear her head. The hum of the highway had left her ears feeling cottony.

"I can do a cartwheel," Annie volunteered. She hopped up and showed him.

"Wow, that was pretty good," Miles said with approval.

"And I can walk over," Annie said, showing him a front and back walk-over.

"You do gymnastics," Miles supplied.

Annie nodded. "It's better when the ground isn't so dirty." She dusted pine needles from her hands. "I can run really fast too."

Lily collected up the plastic wrap and bundled their trash in the bag Eddie had packed their sandwiches in. "You can go down to the jungle gym now, but don't get a stomach ache."

"I won't," Annie shouted gleefully. She sprinted toward the tanbark-covered playground. Lily hurried after her, not wanting to lose sight of her on the overgrown path. She turned to see Miles rise slowly and follow.

"I think it's a good idea if she works off some energy," Lily called back.

He nodded. It must be difficult for him, she realized. He had probably played like this with his own daughter.

Annie had climbed onto the two iron bars to step up to the monkey bars, but she was too short to reach. Lily grabbed her by the hips and lifted her up, and she swung from one to the next with ease. She made it halfway across before dropping to the tanbark and climbing the ladder to try out the slide. She squealed with glee on the way down. Next she hopped onto a swing and Lily got behind her to push.

"Swing your feet when you go forward. That's right. You've got the hang of it."

"This is fun. Push me higher, Aunt Lily!"

Lily experienced an unexpected surge of joy. Annie's happiness was contagious.

Having children had never been important to her. Dating had always been awkward, and once she'd started her own business it had taken up all her time. Because she'd never imagined herself married, naturally she'd never imagined having children. When she'd learned Cassandra had a child even though she wasn't married, Lily had chalked it up to one more extreme thing her wild sister had done. Their mother had raised them with traditional Catholic values, and while Lily was no virgin, she had been a little disappointed with Cassie.

But when she'd met Annie she'd learned instant adoration. The thought of missing out on children of her own simply because no man was interested in her was heartbreaking. She no longer condemned her sister for having a child out of wedlock, and regretted she had.

Miles strolled closer as she pushed Annie on the swing. He leaned against the railing surrounding the playground and scuffed his foot in the tanbark.

Lily ached for him. To know this beautiful joy and then lose it was unimaginable. His pain had to be unbearable.

"Higher! Higher!" Annie squealed with delight.

"I think you're high enough," Lily said.

Miles laughed. The glimpse of happiness brought a surge of warmth to her heart.

Annie jumped off the swing. "Ride the slide with me, Aunt Lily."

"I'll watch you."

"Oh, please. It's so much fun."

Lily climbed the ladder to the wooden platform and slipped into the steel spiral. Thankfully, the structure was built solidly with thick beams and heavy-duty steel. She slid down and hopped off the end laughing, and her elation was tripled by the grin Miles wore.

"I can't tell you the last time I did that," she said as she walked over to him. "Having a kid can make you feel like one again."

Miles' smile faded, and too late Lily realized how insensitive that had been. She glanced at his downcast expression, wishing she could put the happiness back into it.

"I'm sorry."

He shook his head and looked away.

"I realize this is difficult for you. You've made a great sacrifice for us." She leaned against the rail beside him and placed her hand on his where it rested against his hip.

Her heart gave a little leap, as though she'd done something forbidden. His hand was rough, rugged, his masculinity a foreign thing resonating through the sensitive nerve endings in her fingers. Indeed, he felt forbidden, but there was something enticing about the sensation that made her leave her hand there.

"I'm so grateful to you. I can't imagine what might have happened to Annie if you hadn't been there last night."

Now she did move her hand away. To leave it there longer would have been improper, almost suggestive. It was not the impression she wanted to give him.

When he glanced at her his eyes were soft. It was the first time he'd looked at her without suspicion.

"Something's been nagging at me."

Her defenses immediately bristled again. Was this just another cop tactic? She was a fool to think he would ever look at her in a way that wasn't one hundred percent official.

"Last night Annie said they made her sleep in the water. Do you have any idea what she was talking about?"

Lily relaxed. Maybe she'd been hoping for a little more from him, that he might look at her like a woman and not just a victim. Not just another case assignment.

"She's absolutely terrified of the dark. Maybe she had bad dreams. I can't get her to talk much about her life at the compound."

"Did she actually live inside IntelliGenysis?"

Lily shrugged. "I can only guess. If Cassandra owned property or even had personal items in a rented apartment, I think her lawyer would have said something."

"The Ross guy she mentioned in the video?"

Lily nodded. "Doug Ross. He's the one who called me when she died. That's why I didn't know about Annie until I got to Spokane. He assumed I already knew I had a niece and it was a given I would retrieve her."

"Didn't he find your surprise strange?"

She nodded. "But there wasn't anything he could do. One of the documents Cassie had given him was a notarized document naming me her godparent and guardian in the event of an emergency. Colton's name isn't even on Annie's birth certificate. It just says 'unknown' in the section for the father's name." She frowned. "I got the feeling Doug wanted nothing to do with the case."

"Did he give you anything significant? Purse, wallet, diary?"

"Everything he had of Cassandra's fit into a small box. There was a satchel with some documents and her wallet. The wallet had her ATM card, a MasterCard from Scientist's Foundation Credit Union, her driver's license and Social Security card. It seemed like..."

"Like what?"

"She had given him things she wanted to keep safe from Colton; Annie's birth certificate, the notarized document. All her bank statements. Cassandra had sixty-two thousand dollars in a savings account and almost four thousand in her checking. No keys to a house or car. Her driver's license shows Ross and White's address. She had a living trust instead of a will."

Overhead, a helicopter passed across the trees. Its sleek black contours were an ominous sight against the smoke-gray sky. It was far away and continued on, but a bad feeling wove through Lily's stomach.

Annie ran over. "We should go now." She scampered ahead on the trail back to the parking lot. Her sudden decision to leave made a shiver of déjà vu skitter over Lily's flesh. It was almost an exact repeat of the morning in the hotel when Roberta Barker had been killed.

She and Miles started after her. Miles touched Lily in the small of her back as they walked close together on the narrow path.

"Annie said the same thing to me about the water, but she won't explain," Lily told him. "All I know is she doesn't like to take a bath. The shower in the hotel room was the first she'd ever seen, and she insisted on learning to use it by herself."

His hand remained as he helped her up a slight slope. It was such a small gesture, but it revealed the protective nature of this capable man. The disquiet she'd felt vanished.

"When I first met her, I didn't know how much she knew about bathing or dressing herself. I didn't know anything about kids, like at what age they become self-sufficient." She glanced over her shoulder and smiled. "You could say I've had a crash course."

Annie had seemed fairly capable from the start, almost with military precision. Lily wondered if the child's quiet nature was from shyness, or her own crash course in independence. She was so eerily mature, and other than her ignorance of simple things like hamburgers and *Sesame Street*, Lily found Annie's fear of the dark as practically the only childlike quality about her.

Miles returned her smile. "Consider yourself lucky your crash course can talk. When Michelle was a baby she scared the hell out of me. She would cry like the world was coming to an end and I had no idea why."

Miles' face blossomed red and his Adam's apple bobbed in his throat like he'd just swallowed a rock.

Lily turned forward with her own secret smile. That had to have been a difficult memory to relive. The confession had been nice, though, as though she'd earned another notch of his trust.

"Annie can brush her teeth and comb her own hair," Lily told him. "But she didn't know how to tie the laces on the shoes I bought her. If there is one thing I know about kids, they usually learn that before six."

She stepped left and right as the trail took an "S" curve before the parking lot. Her wariness jumped as she realized she couldn't see Annie.

The little girl's scream sent the hair on her nape prickling.

Lily broke into a run but stopped before she got two steps.

A hulking man emerged between the trees, holding Annie in front of him like a shield. His face split into a grin of pure evil. Annie twisted and kicked, screaming for all she was worth.

Time sped up. The man thrust a beefy arm forward. A silver gun with a black, elongated end pointed directly at her. Miles appeared beside her, arms forward. The clicking of his weapon as he thumbed back the hammer ricocheted through her head like breaking glass.

"Put her down!" Miles demanded.

Lily gaped. Her mind skipped over the sight before her, refusing to believe it was truly happening. Her feet were frozen to the ground and she was no longer in control of her own body.

Where time had been moving in blink-fast flashes, now it slowed down like the special effects in a horror movie. Miles shoved her out of the line of fire. The kidnapper's aim swept past her in a wide arc. The gun in his hand bucked once, twice. Puffs of debris exploded in tiny clouds from the sleek, black extension. There was no sound.

In her peripheral vision, she saw Miles dive into the shrubbery.

Annie's scream brought sound back into Lily's world. "You hurt my mommie!" Annie flailed her arms and kicked her heels into the man's stomach, but he didn't even flinch.

The words made no sense. Then they made perfect sense. This was the man who had killed Cassandra.

He aimed at her again. Lily swallowed. Was this her end? She wouldn't run.

"You're not taking her," she said.

The extended barrel pointed straight at her face. He jerked his aim over her head and fired. She winced, but felt nothing.

This time the discharge came with a dull pop.

She stepped forward. His eyes widened in surprise, but his wicked grin increased as though amused by her foolishness.

Lily took another step. Annie fought like a wildcat, but she was no match for this man who stood inhumanly tall. His hands were like baseball gloves, his neck almost as thick as his head.

At her third step, he narrowed his eyes menacingly.

"You can't have her!" Lily's throat burned. She screamed the words. He lifted his hand, and for a frightening moment she thought he would put the muzzle to Annie's head.

The man swung the butt of his gun at her. A blinding light flashed in her eyes and a crack like thunder filled her ears.

Light turned to gray, then to black.

Chapter Eight

"Lily!" Strong hands shook her. Her eyes flashed open. The bright gray sky behind his head sent a spike of pain into her brain. Confusion set in as her vision twisted. She was lying on moist earth pungent with the scent of a recent rain.

Miles. A strange coppery odor. The dull *whuff whuff whuff* of the helicopter, closer now.

The last five days came rushing back. At the forefront of her awareness was a hulking man in black. She bolted upright. "Annie."

Miles yanked her to her feet. They ran through the shrubbery to the parking lot in time to see the helicopter landing at the far end in the area reserved for commercial trucks. The man in black spoke into a radio. Annie flailed, still kicking and thrashing, her bright blond hair whipping in the stir of the chopper's blades.

"Annie! Oh God, *no!*"

She ran, though not knowing what she would do. Jump onto the runner so it couldn't take off, only to be shot off like a clinging insect?

The kidnapper jumped into the unmarked helicopter and it immediately took off. Miles shoved her aside. He took stance and aimed.

"Don't shoot, you'll hit Annie!"

Already the helicopter was lifting away. Lily ran toward it with the absurd hope she could plead them back, that they might take pity on her and return the sweet child. And through she knew that was futile, she continued running anyway when she saw Annie's desperate face peering out at her, hoping to convince the little girl she wouldn't give up, this wasn't the end. She would get her back.

"Annie!" Lily reached toward the sky as the chopper mixed with smoky clouds and the phantom spots swirling across her vision. She fell to her knees sobbing out her anguish.

Miles arrived beside her. Strong arms enveloped her. She smelled his leather jacket, that odd coppery odor, but she saw nothing but the black helicopter fading into the dark sky.

"Annie!" Lily bent forward, seized by sobs. A scream tore through her throat, then another. Miles' grip tightened. The chopper faded away, and there was nothing but the sound of the wind howling through the trees and her pitiful sobbing.

He hauled her to her feet. The world around her dipped and surged. Lily's body felt like rubber.

"We have to move."

"I can't."

"Come on, Lily. I'll help you."

"God, Miles, I lost her. How could I have lost her?"

"You didn't. You stood up to him like a tiger."

The words hardly registered.

"She's gone. Annie's gone."

Her feet dragged as he helped her across the empty parking lot, one arm around her and the other gripping her forearm to keep her upright.

Moments ago there had been a happy family here, with

laughing children who played on the jungle gym, piquing the interest of a sweet, innocent child who had never even seen such a thing. Now the lot was empty except for the Cherokee and a black SUV parked at the far end. No people in sight. It seemed they were the last people on earth. Lily was caught in a surreal science fiction movie, as though she'd fallen asleep with the television on but couldn't wake herself up. This couldn't be real. Things like this didn't happen to normal people.

He pushed her against the side of the Jeep and held her steady as the tears came in great waves and her sobs choked the breath out of her. Miles pulled her against his chest and a strong arm squeezed around her middle.

"Shh, it's all right. Nobody's hurt. The situation is salvageable."

Lily sniffled and pulled away. Contact like this, at this time, was inappropriate. "We have to go back to Spokane. That's where he's taking her."

"Listen to me." He gave her a gentle shake.

Lily glanced at the hole in the arm of his jacket. It was circled by something dark and shiny. *Blood.* What little sanity she had left slipped further away.

"Miles."

"We need to continue to Seattle. We're only an hour away. We'll go straight to the police."

"You're hurt." She reached for the hole in the jacket, pulled it wide and peered inside.

"Easy now." He caught her by the arms and the dark spots in her vision faded.

Lily jerked away. She bent in front of the Jeep and lost the sandwich. Vomiting was horrible, but it was something with which she could identify. Miles came up behind her, touched her back with one hand and held her steady with a firm grip around her forearm with the other, and the minute sliver of control she'd regained vanished.

The memory that she'd wanted his compassion, his trust and even his interest seemed years ago. It was shameful. Annie was in the clutches of a madman because she'd been fantasizing about a man instead of paying attention.

She wiped her mouth with the back of her hand. Lily turned into his grip and received his assessing gaze. His magnificent blue eyes flicked back and forth across each of hers, as if gauging her sanity.

"I'm okay," she assured him. "I'm not afraid of blood. Let me see—how bad is it?"

Miles shook his head. "The guy is a lousy shot, thank God."

"I'll get the first-aid kit." Without waiting for a response, she rounded the Cherokee and opened the back. Only then did she realize it sat askew, all four tires slashed. The nausea returned, rising and falling over her like a wave. Lily swallowed it back. She was not a fragile kitten, useless and blubbering. Now was the time to formulate a plan.

"We know where they're going." She snatched the first-aid kit and unzipped it. "We can be at IntelliGenysis by nightfall."

He touched her shoulder. She glanced up into his pitying eyes. He shook his head.

She turned on him and planted both hands on her hips. At the same instant a new surge of tears sprang into her eyes. "I am *not* going to let him have her."

"We need to go to the police." He spoke calmly. If he'd shouted at her, she could have shouted back. Orders she could have argued with. But the tone he took left no opportunity for disagreement.

"We'll call them from here," she snapped.

Again he shook his head. She glanced over his shoulder at the two public phones. Both handsets had been ripped from their boxes and tossed aside. Her nausea surged and receded. Annie's kidnapper had probably destroyed them with his beefy bare hands.

Miles shrugged out of his coat. He gingerly let it slide off his left arm.

Her decision to leave him and go on her own if he wouldn't comply was dashed in an instant.

This man had been shot for her.

Her eyes filled with new tears. "Oh God, Miles, I'm so sorry."

He grimaced as his jacket fell away. "It isn't your fault."

"The whole *thing* is my fault." She sucked in a breath to force back a sob which escaped anyhow. "If I hadn't left the highway for a smaller road we never would have crashed into your life."

He offered a thin smile and touched her chin. "It wasn't much of a life. You've actually done me a favor."

Lily didn't know what to make of that statement. Rather than try, she took a clean gauze swab and poured some of the antiseptic cleanser into it.

He winced as she touched it to the streak running across the back of his upper arm. "That stings."

"Payback," she said in a pathetic attempt at teasing. The tears wouldn't stop. Maybe she was a blubbering, helpless kitten. She let them fall, concentrating more on keeping the sobs at bay so she could hold a steady hand.

"What are we going to do?"

"We're going to continue to Seattle PD," he told her. "As

planned."

"How? We're stuck here. The cell phones don't work out here."

He glanced past her and she followed his gaze. "He left his car."

"Are you sure it's his?"

It did look like the vehicle that had followed her last night, but she couldn't be sure. All gargantuan SUVs looked alike. But then, who else's would it be?

Lily frowned as she closed up the thin graze with tape sutures. She was confused and only growing more so. "How did he find us?"

"Do you have a cell phone?"

She froze. "I didn't use it."

"It doesn't matter. If it's turned on, it's transmitting a signal."

She closed her eyes. "I feel so stupid."

"Yeah, well, I'm the one who knew better. Colton Reilly probably knows who I am by now. They could have tracked us by either one."

"I don't understand. They don't even work out here. Besides, how would he have access to that kind of information?"

"At this point I wouldn't make any assumptions on how well-equipped Reilly is."

Lily sighed as she fixed a wide bandage across his wound. "I don't know either, but he's rich and at the cutting edge of technology. He's obviously got experts working for him and isn't afraid to break the law." Lily pulled his shirtsleeve back into place. She thought she sounded amazingly coherent, considering her state.

"They probably followed us to the last tower your phone jumped to, and then the chopper found us and told him where to go."

Lily closed her eyes, cursing her ignorance.

"Hey." Miles touched her chin with a finger. "It isn't your fault. You couldn't have known."

She shook her head. "No, Miles. I should have. After all I've been through, I should have known he'd be one step ahead of me."

The corners of his mouth twitched. "After all you've been through, I'd say you're doing pretty damn good."

Lily managed a thin smile in return. Despite his generous praise, the truth was she was barely hanging on.

A lumbering Chevy Suburban pulled into the lot and parked between them and the SUV.

"Thank God." She turned, but Miles grabbed her arm.

"We can't risk endangering civilians."

Lily bit back a choked sob. She hadn't even considered it. "You're right." Frustration tightened in her chest. She'd never felt so helpless or so hopeless.

Miles moved closer. "Just stay cool." She glanced into his eyes. It was the closest she'd been to him. She could smell him, see the tiny gray flecks making his blue eyes such a unique, silvery color, count the pale freckles crossing the bridge of his nose.

A family with two older kids got out to stretch their legs. Thankfully these were teenagers who were too mature to linger on the jungle gym. The older boy wore headphones and ignored the rest of his family. A typical-looking soccer mom jumped out and headed to the restrooms while a teenaged girl trailed behind, protesting for her right to get her tongue pierced.

The father noticed the Cherokee's slashed tires. "Howdy," he called over. "Everything all right?"

Miles smiled and waved. "Yeah, thanks. There are some vandals in the area. We've got a tow truck on the way."

"All right then." He cupped his hands to his mouth and shouted at his wife. "Hey Midge, hurry up."

Miles retrieved his mobile phone from the pocket of his jacket and removed the battery and the SIM card from its back. Lily dug through her ruined purse and did the same.

In five minutes the family of travelers had gone.

"Get your things," Miles told her. He took the first-aid kit by the straps with his good hand and hurried her across the lot to the SUV.

Her suspicions were on high alert and her mind whirled with horrific visions as they drew closer. "What if there's a bomb in it?" She peered through the passenger window as Miles went around to the driver's side. An Enterprise Rent-A-Car fob dangled from the key in the ignition. "He left the key."

"I don't think he'd wire a bomb to the car he was driving, and he couldn't have installed one in the time we've been here." He peered inside and then opened the driver's door. Lily threw her things into the back seat.

"Something's not right with this picture." She grumbled under her breath. "I have a bad feeling."

"Do you want to go behind the trees while I start it up?"

She frowned. "You're missing the point. I don't want you to blow up either."

Miles dropped to his hands and knees to check the undercarriage, and then carefully checked the interior front and back, but she sensed he was doing it mostly to appease her.

Lily climbed in. She fastened her seatbelt with eyes closed

as Miles started the engine, counting to ten before she was convinced they weren't going to explode.

"Check the glove compartment," he told her.

She snatched out the folded contract. "It's in the name of Vince Johnson."

Her hope soared, but Miles dashed it by shaking his head. "Ten-to-one it's not his real name."

He was probably right. A kidnapper and killer wouldn't rent a car in his own name.

Miles shifted into reverse and backed them out of the parking space.

"Maybe I should drive," she said when she saw him turn the wheel one-handed.

"No offense, but I don't think you're in good enough condition."

They pulled onto the highway. Lily stared down at her hands in her lap. He was right. She was a wreck, and she'd probably *cause* a wreck.

The SUV was newer than the Cherokee and more thoroughly insulated from the road. The silence inside the luxurious leather interior was painful. Lily itched to get out. She imagined she could smell the hulking hit man's odor mingling with the new leather.

She replayed the horrific scene over and over until her head hurt and her stomach swam. Then she pictured Cassandra's face in her mind and it only got worse.

She'd failed her sister. She'd failed Annie. And she'd failed herself.

Clouds blackened the sky and fat rain drops spattered the windshield as they reached the city limits. It was after six. Miles wondered if his old boss would even still be in.

Lily had been silent the whole way. Several glances in her direction confirmed his suspicions. She was in shock.

She finally spoke when they pulled to a stop at a red light in Seattle. "I would have made a lousy mother."

"That's not true. That wasn't your ordinary situation."

"Doesn't matter. I failed it anyway."

He reached over and cupped her hand. It was like ice. "You stood up to a man with a gun."

"Plain old stupidity. I'm no good to Annie dead."

"Sweetheart, don't be so hard on yourself."

She snorted. "You called me sweetheart." She laughed again, a pitiful, desperate sound, then covered her face with her hand as her laughter turned to sobs.

His worry leapt another notch. She was losing it. She'd been through so much in the past two days he was surprised she didn't need a padded room.

He took Madison to Pike Street and pulled into the side lot at Seattle's East Precinct. He turned off the engine and swiveled toward her in the seat. "Can you keep it together?"

Lily wiped her cheeks and sat up straighter in the seat. "I have to, for Annie."

He jumped out and rounded the car to help her. Lily took his outstretched hand and slid out.

Forgotten sensations raced through him as their fingers connected and held. It felt strange to comfort and protect a woman again. Lily wasn't the only one feeling the shock of facing a man with a gun. The day's events had brought his nerve endings alive again, and every sensation was like a bolt of electricity straight into his brain.

Long-ago memories snapped to life in his mind's eye.

Everything about the small station looked exactly the same, from the chief's name etched in the glass on the front doors to the scarred linoleum floor and solid oak desk in the precinct's front lobby.

Then a dreadful moment lingered when a sea of unfamiliar faces stared back at him.

"Yes, can I help you?" asked a woman who looked fresh out of high school.

Miles opened his mouth to ask for Billings when Detective Crawford's voice boomed above the busy office area, as loud and obtrusive as always. "Hey, Montana, look who's here." Crawford's cheer faded when he got a good look at Miles.

"We need to see Chief Billings. It's an emergency."

"Yeah, yeah, come inside. It's okay, Maggie. This guy would'a had my job if he'd stuck around."

The woman at the desk hit a buzzer and Detective Crawford held the gate to the office area open for them. "What brings you back to this hellhole?"

"There's been a kidnapping," Lily blurted. "A six-year-old girl has been taken."

Though he was known to be crass at times, Miles was grateful Crawford's face showed the proper concern.

"Your daughter?"

"My niece."

Joe "Montana" White came over and Miles introduced her to both men.

"What's going on Miles? You look like hell."

"It's been a helluva two days." He ran a hand over his face, feeling the bristle on his chin.

Montana seated them in Billing's office. Miles rose again immediately when Billings entered and clasped his former boss's hand.

"Miles, what's it been, three years?"

Miles nodded. "Chief Billings, this is Lily Brent. She's had a run in with Colton Reilly."

"That wacko from the Twilight Zone? No offense, ma'am." He gestured to Detective White. "Get some coffee into these two. They look half-dead."

Miles nearly laughed. He'd been half-dead for the last three years. In the last two days he'd felt more alive than he ever remembered.

Montana went for the coffee as Miles took his seat again. Everything about the office was exactly the same, right down to the old leather guest chairs, except now there was an autographed photo of Billings with Jake Woods of the Mariners on the wall.

Miles started by recounting everything he knew down to the trip to the Parkmont police station. He left out the weird stuff, not entirely sure it had really happened. He was certain he'd imagined his vision of Annie last night, and he'd written off Eddie's strange reaction to the girl as overexertion. The only thing he knew had really happened was the incident with the deer this morning, but in truth that hadn't been so odd.

"I had to take the truck," Miles finished. "It's parked in your lot."

Billings nodded. "We'll impound it and notify the rental company." He'd listened to the entire story without a change in his expression. "Do you have a copy of the video tape?"

Lily opened her purse and handed it over.

"May I?"

She nodded.

Miles noted the hopeful look on her face. Billings was not

doing a lot to assure her the National Guard would be called to raid IntelliGenysis, as she was probably hoping.

"Is there anything you want to add to this?"

She glanced at him and Miles touched her hand. A tiny smile found her lips. "Miles pretty much covered it all."

"You didn't see anything at the hotel in Spokane?"

She shook her head.

"All right." Billings pushed back from his desk and stood. "Crawford, are the paramedics here yet for our drunk and disorderly?"

Detective Crawford shouted a confirmation from the outer room.

"Miles, why don't you come with me and give a gunshot report, and we'll have them take a look at your arm." Chief Billings nodded at Lily. "Detective White will keep you company, Ms. Brent."

Miles knew Billings wanted to speak to him alone. From the frown Lily tossed sideways, she knew it too.

Chapter Nine

Billings remained silent as one of the paramedics checked Miles' arm.

"Is this lady a fifty-one-fifty?" he finally asked.

"I don't think so," Miles said. Lily definitely wasn't nuts. She was one of the strongest and most courageous women he'd ever met.

The paramedic pressed the bandage back down. "Unless you want stitches, it's fine as is."

"No thanks," Miles told him. He hopped off the desk, pulling his shirtsleeve back into place as he followed Billings into the viewing room. The chief plugged the video in.

Seeing it again made Miles' blood turn to ice. He noticed desperate nuances in Cassandra Brent's eyes he hadn't seen the first time. He felt the panic, recognized the hopelessness. The woman knew she was dying and understood she was making an outrageous request of Lily, but as a mother she was desperate to find safety for her child.

Miles ran a hand through his hair. Watching Annie get taken had nearly killed him. It was like his own daughter dying all over again. Even though he relived her death in his mind every single day, Annie's abduction had brought back a pain so vivid and sharp he could hardly stand it. It was a miracle he'd come away from the rest stop with his sanity still intact.

Maybe it was his rage with Reilly's henchman keeping him going. This man had to be stopped. A small part of him had expected a standoff, but the man had fired on him without warning. Miles couldn't shoot the perp without risking Annie. Now he wished he had taken the shot.

One thing he knew for certain, he couldn't just dump Lily here. There was no backing out now. As painful as it was to be near Lily and Annie, he could never live with himself for walking away from her.

This child could be saved.

"Jesus Christ," Billings said as the grisly scene ended.

"That's the same thing Noah said, more or less."

"He's seen it?"

"I was there this morning."

Billings rose from his chair and hit the rewind button. "I'd like a copy of this for evidence."

Miles nodded. "I'm sure Lily will sign a release."

Billings punched the buttons to start the copy process. The scene replayed as it copied to a second machine. They both looked away, as though Billings couldn't bear to see it again either. Miles didn't need to. Cassandra Brent's voice echoed in his mind, permanently etched there.

"This must be hard for you."

"You have no idea."

"I know what you're thinking. I know you, Miles. It may have been three years, but I still know you. You don't have any obligation to this woman. You can turn her over to us."

Miles didn't comment. The tape turned to static and Billings ejected it. He offered it, but held fast as Miles grasped it.

"This isn't proof. Something like this could easily be faked.

I don't want to see you get caught up in something bad because you've got a need to help that comes...not from your head."

"Whether you're talking about my heart or my dick, you're wrong either way."

Billings barked out a laugh.

"I brought her here, didn't I?"

The Chief's frown slid back into place as he released the video. "It's what happens after you leave I'm worried about."

Miles grinned. "You sound exactly like Noah. Consider me twice warned."

Miles came back to the office alone.

Not a moment too soon, Lily thought. Detective White's awkward attempts at small talk were limited to football and the precinct's lousy coffee.

She'd begun to feel shaky and unsure and the sight of Miles' handsome face eased away the chill that had settled under her skin. She pushed out of her chair as he walked back into the office. He handed back the tape, a silent indication they weren't going anywhere yet.

"What did he say?"

"They're checking out your story."

"Another cop who wants to check out my story. How long is this going to take?"

"Ms. Brent, Chief Billings used to be with the Justice Department," Detective White explained. "He's the best in the state. You're in good hands."

"Well, unfortunately Annie isn't. She's in a madman's hands, as a matter of fact. Taken at gunpoint. Time is critical."

"As is procedure. There is a right way to handle things like this."

"Yeah, like put out an *Amber* alert."

"Lily," Miles cut in, "you and I both know she's already back at IG."

"Then get a warrant and go in and get her." She enunciated the words slowly. Why did everyone around her suddenly seem stupid? The two men were looking at her like she was insane. From Miles, it hurt. He of all people should know the urgency of the situation. He had seen it all with his own eyes. He'd been shot, for God's sake.

The chief entered the office and Lily perched on the edge of her chair. "Chief Billings, what do you intend to do?"

He sat and let out a long sigh. The SUV's rental agreement landed on his desk. He tossed a black and white printout of a mug shot down and flipped it so Lilly could see it.

"That's him," she said immediately.

"The first thing I'm going to do is put out a warrant on your shooter. Vince Johnson is really Vincent Luggo, a bounty hunter out of Los Angeles. He's had several arrests, various charges indicating he's aggressive, but nothing leading to a pattern. By that I mean he's not a drug dealer, not a thief, just a thug."

Lily waited tensely. It sounded like good news, but it wasn't the news she wanted to hear. "He killed my sister."

"We don't have any proof of that."

"Except your only living eyewitness identified him," she tossed back. "When he grabbed her, Annie said he was the man who hurt her mother."

"And that will certainly be taken into consideration when an arrest is made. Right now we can only take him for weapons charges, kidnapping and attempted murder, but that should be enough."

"Is it enough to get into IntelliGenysis?"

Billings shook his head. "Unfortunately not. We have nothing to tie him to Colton Reilly's organization."

Lily looked at Miles, silently willing him to say something to make a difference to these men.

"Your video checks out with the Spokane police department. It was filmed at Sacred Heart General where your sister passed." He looked down at his notepad. "An officer Dwight Markham signed off your sister's personal effects to you on Monday the fifteenth."

"I could have told you all that."

"Ms. Brent, we need to verify all the facts before we can take action."

"I can't believe this. We're talking about a kidnapping here. The man tried to kill us."

"We don't have any proof Vince Luggo is affiliated with Colton Reilly or IntelliGenysis. The helicopter that picked him up bore no markings. Additionally, at this time, legal custody of the child hasn't been established. You said Colton Reilly is her father, you hadn't seen your sister in years. Before we can act we need legal proof Cassandra Brent had custody of the child she removed from Colton Reilly's care. Ms. Brent, you said yourself you didn't even know your sister had a child. Is it possible—"

"No, it isn't possible," she interrupted. "You're about to insinuate Cassie took a child she had no right to? Did you even watch her video? She died trying to protect Annie."

Miles placed a hand on her shoulder. "Lily, we saw it. No one is disputing she was desperate to save Annie."

She was grateful he was here with her, but the gesture was

an insulting request to calm down. These men didn't appear to feel the urgency. Obviously she wasn't riled enough.

A young black woman poked her head in the door. Billings waved her in.

"I just got off the phone with Child Protective Services. The supervisor who would know more about Annie Brent's case has already gone home for the day, but the girl in the office checked the computer. No paperwork has been filed regarding a transfer of custody." She glanced at her notepad. "And no luck reaching the lawyer. I've left a message with the answering service for Ross and White. They assure me he's good about answering urgent pages after hours."

Billings smiled at the young officer. "Thank you, Denise."

Lily's heart sank. It was one roadblock after another. "You're not going to do anything."

"There is nothing I can do. I'm limited by legal constraints. I can't just storm into IntelliGenysis with guns blazing." He smiled as if it was a joke that should make her laugh. Rationally, she knew he was right, but it didn't make it any easier to accept.

"I'm going to post a patrol car outside your home tonight. I would suggest hiring a lawyer, Ms. Brent. I would also suggest you take a trip to Spokane as soon as you're able. You're wanted for questioning. Roberta Barker's death has been classified as murder."

She gasped, horrorstruck.

He held up a hand. "You aren't a suspect, but you were involved. The hotel staff verified you met with her in the hotel's conference room the night of her death, and you two had switched rooms. In fact, they thought it was you they'd found until the police identified her by her driver's license."

Lily chewed her lip. Things had gone from bad to worse.

"It doesn't sit well that you left before the on-duty could question you."

"An employee delivering room service saw her attacker run out of the room." Lily was surprised she could speak. This was all going horribly wrong, and she worried it would conclude with her being photographed front and profile. "Will he be shown a picture of Vince Luggo?"

"Yes, he will. But until we find something to link him with Reilly, it won't give us probable cause to serve IntelliGenysis with a warrant."

"I don't believe this." She shoved back in her chair with an angry grumble.

"Ms. Brent, I know this might sound indifferent, but you need to trust me on this—you don't want us to risk doing anything rash. A mistake made by the police could hurt your case in the long run."

The man's face softened but it did nothing to ease her angst.

"I feel for you and the little girl, truly I do. I'm a father and a grandfather, and I can't begin to imagine what you're going through. I promise you I'll do whatever I can to investigate this matter and try to find a solution to help Annie. And regardless of all else, rest assured we are going to do everything within our power to keep you safe."

"It's not me you should be worried about. Annie hated being there. She was terrified of Colton Reilly. They were doing something bad to her." She lifted her hands and clenched her fists in frustration. "What kind of a person would send a vicious brute to steal a child at gunpoint?"

"You might be surprised."

She glanced at Miles. His face was a mask of granite. She was sure these men had seen horrors in their line of work, but right now she could conceive of no greater horror than what had happened to Annie.

"Ms. Brent, if you have the funds, I suggest you hire the best lawyer available. My daughter is currently going through a divorce and suing for custody of her two kids. Her situation isn't all that messy, but nevertheless it's been a nightmare. You're up against one of the wealthiest men in the state who obviously isn't afraid to push the bar. You're in for a battle, and you need to arm yourself appropriately."

Lily felt as rubbery as a deflated balloon. She and Miles sat in silence in the back seat of the squad car for the twenty-minute trip to her townhouse.

Fat, lazy raindrops beat down steadily, trailing in rivulets over the car's windows. The city lights were transformed into a blurry kaleidoscope of color, making Seattle look unfamiliar and strange. She turned to stare out her window, hiding the silent tears streaming down her cheeks.

Miles grasped her hand and wove his fingers within hers. The gesture was so surprising she gasped. She wiped her cheeks with one hand while she held firmly on to him with the other.

"I'm sorry." Almost no sound came as he said it, but the words were still so vibrant they resounded in her head.

She managed a shaky smile. "You shouldn't be." This poor man carried so much on his shoulders.

"It's going to be all right."

She sighed, defeated, but nodded. He gave her hand a reassuring squeeze.

The rest of the ride finished in silence, but it was a few precious moments of tender peace she wished she could put in her pocket and relive at a better time, when all her worries were gone and Annie was safe.

The officer pulled into Rose Crest and turned right and left where she indicated. He parked at the curb in front of her townhouse.

The officer went inside while they waited in the entry. Miles shifted close and did a slow exploration of her face. The way his eyes roamed over her lips, chin and neck was like a sexual caress.

"I need to call your alarm company and inform them of the situation," the officer said from the living room. "Even though I'm here, they should treat any alarm with the utmost priority."

Lily led them to the kitchen. She dialed the cordless phone and cradled it against her shoulder while she started the coffee maker. When the alarm company came on the line she gave them her password and handed over the handset.

Miles settled onto a bar stool at the kitchen island as the officer spoke. Lily took a bottle of water from the refrigerator and chased down two aspirin.

The officer hung up the phone. "We're set. Ms. Brent, I'd like you to keep the curtains closed and please don't leave the house without telling me."

She raised her hands in surrender. "I'm not going anywhere."

The crisp sound of the heavy downpour disappeared behind the door. Lily punched the buttons on the keypad. Each beep rang shrilly loud in her overtired ears. Then there was nothing but the muffled patter of rain all around them.

It struck her at that moment that she was about to have a man spend the night for the first time. She guessed the situation wasn't unusual for most people, but for her it was. She was suddenly very aware of his raw masculinity, the deep intensity of those magical blue eyes, and his powerful sexual energy.

As though he could read her mind, he asked, "Do you want me to get a hotel room for the night?"

"No, of course not." She started past him, embarrassed. Could he see her bashfulness so clearly? "It's after nine and it's pouring out."

Lily stalked into her living room practically running, then turned abruptly and faced him. She willed herself to stop the jerky movements, but she felt like an awkward teenager.

He followed her slowly. "I think it would be better."

"Nonsense. I'll get you a pair of sweats I think you'll fit into, and I'll show you where the washer and dryer are."

She hurried upstairs to dig out a soft, baggy sweat suit he could squeeze into. Once back in the living room, she handed them over with the flannel shirt he'd loaned her and led the way down to the second suite. She opened the door and threw it wide.

"The laundry nook is down here." She continued down the narrow steps. The machines sat in a small recess before the door to the garage. A basket of towels sat on the machine waiting to be washed. "Just dump your clothes in here and this'll make a full wash."

She faced him in the narrow hall. "Help yourself to anything in the kitchen. I'll make us something to eat in the morning before we go."

"Go?" He stopped her with a hand on her arm. He could see her nervousness, and that made it a hundred times worse.

"I'm going to rent a car and head back to Spokane. Chief Billings said I should go as soon as possible. I can take you home on the way."

He frowned as if he knew she was planning something entirely different. His suspicious gaze lingered for a long minute. He sighed, realizing there was nothing he could say to stop her.

"I'm going to make a call about the Jeep."

"There's a phone in your room."

Once alone in the kitchen, she breathed out her tension in a long sigh. Miles set her every nerve on edge. He was right, staying here wasn't the best idea, but she couldn't very well turn him out now. He would never understand she was a shy, super nerd who'd never had a serious relationship and fell to pieces in the presence of a halfway decent-looking guy.

And in Miles' case, that meant she was completely shattered. He was more than halfway decent looking. He was two-hundred percent spectacular masculinity.

Lily poured herself a cup of coffee and headed to her office. She booted up her computer and settled into her comfy office chair.

An internet search of IntelliGenysis brought up the typical multitude of results. At first it looked like a lot, considering the secrecy of the organization, but Lily was disappointed to find most of them were of the company's own vague website and random press releases about inconsequential things.

By the time her coffee was cold she was no closer to understanding what was going on at IntelliGenysis or how Annie could possibly be involved.

Finally, she came to a New York Times article about Baxall Laboratories that mentioned IntelliGenysis. She followed the link to the article, a press release about a scientist hired by Baxall as their new head of research and development. A photo revealed a pretty Asian woman named Meiling Wong. Lily skimmed the article for the reference to IntelliGenysis.

Baxall Laboratories announced today Meiling Wong has been hired as Director of Research and Development for their drug division. Wong is most noted for a 2002 Nobel Prize nomination for her drug RH24, a revolutionary chemical compound that splices out certain defect-causing genes from a patient's genetics.

Wong is confident gene splicing drugs will eventually eradicate most, if not all, inheritable diseases from our genetic makeup.

"Imagine a world where young people study diseases in history class, not biology," Wong says. "Genetic engineering has the potential to eradicate defects in the gene pool and forever remove almost every type of inherent defect, everything from Alzheimer's to congenital heart disease. Even baldness. I believe our generation is about to see astounding changes in medicine as radical as the advent of the automobile was to our great-grandparents."

Wong has devoted her life to genetic studies. She completed her doctorate at Stanford University and did her residency at Stanford Research Institute in Palo Alto, California. She comes to Baxall from a five-year position at IntelliGenysis, where her work was responsible for revolutionary breakthroughs in juvenile disease research.

Lily's heart leapt. If she could just talk to this woman, she might be able to learn what was going on at IntelliGenysis. She printed the article and then clicked on the contact link to discover Baxall was located in Washington's premier research area.

"What are you doing?"

She started and bumped her cup, spilling cold coffee on her

desk. Miles stood in the doorway. His hair was damp and tousled and his skin was freshly scrubbed.

Absurdly, she wondered if this was what he looked like every morning. Her skin grew warm. He looked good enough to eat.

"What's this?" He snatched the paper out of the printer on the stand by the doorway.

She braced herself for a lecture as he scanned the paper. His heavy-lidded eyes rose to hers, making her gulp. He almost looked resigned, as if he had expected her to be up to no good.

"She'll have answers," Lily said defensively. Why did this man have the power to uproot the confidence she'd worked so hard to develop as an adult?

Because he's the most gorgeous creature I've ever seen, and he leapt to my rescue like a knight in shining armor.

She didn't wait for a response. He wasn't her keeper. He could hardly stop her from speaking to the woman. Tomorrow she was going to drive him home and she would never see him again.

Her throat tightened at the thought, but she hardly had time to dwell on it now. Rescuing Annie was the single most important priority in her life. She swallowed away the regret as she pointed her browser to a popular online yellow pages and entered a search for Meiling Wong.

The paper crinkled as he lowered his hand, but Lily didn't look up. She found a listing for Meiling Wong in South Manning, then pasted the address into a map site and printed out the results.

"Are you going to go marching up to her demanding answers?"

"Something like that." Lily gave him a cautious smile. "I'll be nice."

"I'm sure you will," Miles said. "But I doubt you're going to get the answers you want." He snatched the second page from the printer, glanced at it and handed them both to her.

"That's for me to worry about." Lily shut down the computer and stood, feeling like they'd suddenly become strangers.

In truth, that was all they were. And though she had probably imagined whatever tenderness she'd glimpsed between them, the sudden chilliness hurt.

He remained in the doorway, and the stare he returned was assessing. *He's being a cop again,* she thought. *Expecting I'm going to do something he wouldn't approve of.*

Well, let him. She didn't owe him any explanation. It wasn't his child that had been taken.

She drew a deep breath. She was cranky, and though private, her thoughts were nasty. The man had lost his child. His little girl was gone forever. Lily couldn't begin to imagine the pain consuming his soul.

And she did owe him. She owed him her very life.

"Did you find everything you need?" she asked in a softer voice. He must have. He'd shaved and smelled slightly minty.

He nodded. "Thanks."

"Good night, then."

How easy it would be to step forward into his arms. His entire body looked primed to take her in an embrace.

Again, she was imagining it. Her exhausted mind was playing tricks on her, letting her see what she longed for.

Chapter Ten

Miles sprawled across the middle of the king-size guest bed, his body bone weary but his eyes wide open.

He hadn't for a moment expected Lily would sit back and let the police handle this. She was desperate to retrieve Annie. Recklessly so. The woman was going to get herself killed.

She was no fool. This palatial townhouse and the fat portfolio of graphic designs for international clientele on the living room coffee table was proof of that. Her kitchen was right out of Better Homes and Gardens. The last time he'd seen so much steel, granite and glass, he'd been in the San Francisco Museum of Modern Art.

But as savvy as she might be, Lily wasn't thinking clearly. She was exhausted and in shock, liable to make a tragic mistake.

His mind replayed the kidnapping over and over, each time with painfully bright clarity.

Had the tragic mistake been his?

If he'd taken the shot would Vince Luggo be dead? Would Annie be safely tucked into this bed instead of him? Would Colton Reilly be without his henchman and forced to slink back to his freakish compound with his tail between his legs?

Or would Lily be mourning the death of an innocent little

girl she never had the chance to know?

Had he hesitated because he'd lost his nerve?

Everything was out of whack because of Lily. Every molecule in his body screamed to get the hell out of here. He wanted to go back to his dreary little house and cocoon himself in his dreary little world so badly his skin itched.

When Chief Billings said Spokane PD first believed it was Lily who'd died in the hotel room, he felt as if he'd taken a punch to the gut. The idea of Lily lying on a coroner's slab turned each beat of his heart into a painful kick against the walls of his chest.

Those were dangerous feelings.

Miles shot to his feet and strode from the room. He needed a glass of water. Hell, he needed a stiff drink.

At many of the electrical outlets, crystal-faceted nightlights threw sparkly circles of light, making the townhouse glow. Michelle had been afraid of the dark, though not on the same level as Annie. She had adored all things magically Disney and would have loved these soft, welcoming lights. Miles preferred the darkness. To him this was just another indication of Lily's sweetness, another reminder he didn't need of the charm of this special woman.

The marble tiles of the kitchen floor were cold against his feet, grounding him in reality. He opened the refrigerator and found a casserole dish with half a homemade lasagna covered in plastic. She'd made it cheesy, with a bubbly-browned top. He removed the dish, found a fork and ate it cold. Because of the tension he'd experienced all day, he hadn't realized he was hungry, but now the food made his stomach come back to life.

He went back to the refrigerator, grabbed a pear and a loaf of bread to make a peanut butter and jelly sandwich. The jars were an organic brand with no preservatives, artificial colors or flavors. Lily would provide well for Annie. She would build a loving, healthy home in which to raise a child.

Anything would be better than being raised inside the IG compound, but somehow he knew life with Lily would be extra special.

He ate in silence and cleaned up the kitchen all in the glow of those faceted nightlights. There was a homey, almost Christmas-like quality about them that brought a melancholy ache to his heart.

With his belly full, Miles padded across the plush living room carpeting to the stairs leading down but stopped, having forgotten the pear. He should put it back in the refrigerator.

He turned around and stopped dead in his tracks. Annie stood in the center of the living room.

His heart leapt into a rapid staccato.

She was dressed in a black spandex body suit covering her from wrists to neck to ankles. Her hair was pulled back in a ponytail, fixed at the nape of her neck.

She looked like a phantom, pale and solemn and without the cheerful vivacity she'd displayed even at her most sedate times at the cabin. The child who had been overly enthusiastic about canned stew had been replaced by a ghostly, miserable-looking urchin. Her eyes were deep-set and shadowed, her mouth drawn.

Miles couldn't move, could hardly breathe. He was so certain he'd imagined her first appearance he'd completely wiped it from his mind.

Now he knew with certainty...*this child has special powers.*

"There aren't any cameras on the roof, Mr. Miles."

Finally the breath he'd been desperate for raced into his lungs. In the blink of an eye, all incredulity was gone.

Annie is special. Simple as that.

"Don't touch the fences."

"Where are you, Annie?"

"I'm in the water."

Jesus, she can hear me. "Are you hurt?"

"I don't like it here. You're coming for me, aren't you?" Her voice softened with fearful hesitation, and the raw desperation in it ripped him in two.

"Yes, we're coming. There are lots of people coming. You hang in there, okay?"

"Mr. Reilly is really angry."

Her image dissolved into silvery ripples as though she was underwater and someone had disturbed the surface.

"I miss you, Aunt Lily."

The last shimmery traces disappeared completely.

"Annie!" Lily's scream made him spin around. She stood stiffly at the base of the steps, a white-knuckled grip on the wooden handrail. She wore a cotton nightshirt that stopped above her knees and her hair was a sexy tousle of sleep-rumpled curls.

Her frightened eyes flicked to him, then to the darkness of the living room behind him. She rushed forward. "Annie!"

Miles caught her around the waist and hauled her against him. He felt her softness through the thin cotton nightshirt and nearly groaned out loud. A plump breast brushed against his arm. The curve of her thigh mingled with his. It was nearly his undoing.

She was unsteady on her feet, staring into the darkness where Annie had been. Her chest heaved with panicked breaths, her face a mixture of horror, confusion and desperation. He tightened his grip, acutely aware of every soft inch of her body touching his.

"She isn't here, Lily."

"But...I saw her."

"I did too."

Her gaze snapped to him. Against his will, his heart went out to her.

"Have you ever seen her do that before?"

Lily's horrified eyes widened. "What? No! My God."

"Last night she appeared to me." A chill rolled over his flesh at the memory. Annie had said she wanted to see them. She was either astute enough to know, or by some ungodly miracle she had known, Sara had died too.

"What do you mean?"

He looked at the empty void Annie had occupied. "Just like that."

"Miles." His name rushed out of her on a panicked breath. He brought her in front of him and held her firmly by both arms.

"You said she was special. What did you mean?"

Her gaze slipped away. She moistened her lips with her tongue. His body responded without his consent.

"Lily." He gave her a small shake. "You've got to tell me what you know."

She shook her head, still dazed. "Intuitive. That's all. Just little things, though, that I could never put my finger on. Like the deer."

The deer. And Eddie's strange episode, followed by a sudden and significant improvement in his health. He glanced at the glowing face of a digital clock by the kitchen table. If he thought Eddie's cell phone would work at the cabin, Miles would call him, even though it was midnight.

Midnight. Last night he'd glanced at the clock at eleven fifty-eight, and not two minutes later he'd seen Annie.

As Lily's eyes met his the confusion gave way to misery. "Why did she look like that?"

"She looked wet." Miles realized he was squeezing her arms, holding her stiffly in front of him. He relaxed his grip and eased her over to the couch. "It makes sense. Remember—she said they make her sleep in the water."

"My God. What are they doing to her?"

Lily sagged against him. He collected her in an embrace that felt much too natural. She tucked her long legs beneath her as she leaned into him and wrapped her arms around him.

For a moment he sat in dumbfounded silence, searching for a nice way to ask her to move.

But he didn't. One hand hesitantly touched her back and then the other found it easier to caress the curtain of soft hair falling over his chest. Lily trembled under his touch, and her embrace tightened.

His body responded with an ache so primal it shamed him, yet felt magnificent and necessary, like a breath drawn after too long underwater.

He would never betray Sara's memory with the physical need for another woman, but forces outside his control had brought them together in this bizarre situation, and his every nerve was reacting to it with explosive need.

Something incredible was happening here, something he would no longer fight. There was time for atonement later.

And he'd made a promise to a little girl. Across some supernatural plane he couldn't explain, he'd made a promise.

"God, Miles, I'm scared." She leaned away and looked into

his eyes. Hers shimmered with tears.

"I'm a little freaked out myself." He mustered a smile for her sake. "At least we know she's all right."

Lily jerked back. "We know nothing of the sort. Did you see that? She could be dead for all we know. That could have been her ghost."

He tightened his grip on her arm. Lord forgive him, he wished she would lean back against him again. "I don't think so. Lily, I saw the same thing last night and she was fine afterward. I don't think she even remembered it."

Her expression crumbled. "What did you see?"

"She appeared in front of me. I think she moved something with her mind." He told her about the events the night before, watching her eyes widen in shock.

"Did she say anything?"

He swallowed. "She said she wanted to see them. She'd turned the photo of my family upright."

Lily glanced away and eased back on the couch, widening the gap between them.

"Tonight..." He swallowed over the sudden discomfort clogging his throat. "I spoke to her and she responded. Did you see?"

She nodded. "I heard her say Colton was angry and she missed me." Lily's attention perked. "What else did she say?"

He repeated what she'd said, but didn't tell Lily about Annie's heart-wrenching plea. She already knew Annie didn't want to be there, and it would only upset her to hear it.

"Now do you see why we have to speak to this scientist?" She threw him a pointed look. "I need to know what's going on."

Miles agreed, but the incident was making him think this was out of his league. Bad guys with guns he was trained handle, psychic phenomenon he was not.

Lily sagged against the back of the couch. A wisp of hair brushed across his forearm. She brought one hand to her face. "I don't know what to do. I feel so helpless. A real parent would know what to do."

"Nobody can accuse you of not trying." He swiveled toward her on the couch and Lily eased back against him. Before he could consciously stop himself, he took her in his arms. She fit against him like a puzzle piece that belonged and a warm rush of comfort surged through him.

"I've got to get her out of there," she said on a sigh. Her body relaxed. She was warm against him, pliant and soft and perfectly feminine. Miles couldn't remember the last time he'd allowed himself even the basest pleasure. He never languished in a hot shower anymore, couldn't remember the last time he'd eaten a piece of pie, hadn't even joined his buddies for a beer and a game of pool in years.

It would be easy to lose himself in Lily's lush beauty. Easy to close his eyes, breathe her in, let his hands roam over her.

But Lily was hovering on the edge of shock for the third time in as many days. To take her now would be to take advantage of her vulnerability. As much as he flirted with the idea of enjoying her body without an emotional connection, he was not the kind of man who treated a woman that way.

Besides, the emotional connection was already there. There was no denying it. He cared about Lily.

They remained in each other's arms until she gave a deep breath in and out, and he realized she'd fallen asleep. He eased her over and scooped her up.

The floor plan upstairs was the same as the master suite downstairs, but where the guestroom was austere, Lily's bedroom was warm with a cream and pink floral country pattern. He hadn't expected this of her. The rest of her townhouse was almost severe in its modernism, yet this soft and feminine bedroom revealed more about the sweetness of the pretty woman in his arms.

Her bed was rumpled as though she'd also tried, but couldn't sleep. He eased her onto the mattress. She moved her lips and a soft mewling sound escaped.

Miles stood back and looked at her. The cotton sleep shirt had ridden up her thighs, giving him an unobstructed view of those long, slender legs. Her nipples pressed against the thin fabric. He could barely make out the dark circles of her areolas through the thin fabric.

He drew a ragged breath and dragged his hand through his hair. A gentle breeze of roses and lemon floated up to him as he pulled the blankets over her.

With the blood rushing through his ears, Miles quietly slipped out of the room and headed back downstairs.

This was too much for him. Had his body not needed relief so badly he might be better prepared to handle this situation. But Lily was a beautiful woman with a sensual nature and a very sexy body, and Miles couldn't think straight when he was around her.

That meant he was no good to her, no good to Annie and no good to himself.

Chapter Eleven

Lily heard the shower downstairs as she was preparing breakfast. She hurried around her kitchen awkwardly, both because she wasn't used to cooking for a guest and because she still felt slightly uncomfortable about the previous night.

She'd awakened in his arms as he carried her upstairs, but Lily had kept her eyes squeezed shut as a torrent of unfamiliar emotions kicked and bruised her.

She couldn't help but be attracted to Miles. He was as gorgeous as the magazine cover models she worked with in her designs. But in his mind, Miles was still married to another woman, and even as inexperienced with men as she was, Lily knew there was no competing with a memory.

She looked up to find Miles in the archway. His shirt was unbuttoned and his hair left to dry in a curly halo around his face. He was in need of a trim, but it looked downright sexy on him. He really could double for one of the cover models whose photos scattered her desk at work.

"Good morning." Her voice sounded thick. "I've got breakfast on."

"It smells great. Did I hear someone at the door?"

"I had a rental car delivered," she said simply. She felt his eyes on her as he followed.

She poured batter onto the hot griddle in the island as Miles took a stool on the opposite side. She poured him a cup of coffee and served him a bowl of sliced fruit. He buttoned his shirt before eating, hiding away his glorious chest.

She accidentally bit her tongue. Goodness, what was wrong with her? *Focus, Lily. Annie needs you to concentrate.*

"You have a nice kitchen. The whole place is nice. You'll make a good home for Annie."

His voice sounded thick too. Was he as uncomfortable about last night as she was? He'd put her into bed wearing only a threadbare t-shirt. She should have thought more carefully about her choice of nightclothes.

"You sound confident I'll get her back." She looked into his eyes for an indication he believed it.

"Have you thought about what you'll do after you do?"

"What do you mean?" She flipped the pancakes. They landed wet side down with a sizzle and immediately rose with tiny curls of steam.

Miles dropped his gaze and dug into the fruit as though he needed to think about how to convey his thoughts without making her upset. He didn't realize the delay tactic itself put her on edge.

"Maybe you should consider professional help."

Her already rising hackles shot up.

"You've got to admit, she's not your ordinary kid."

"She's an innocent little girl," Lily replied evenly. She took a sip of tea, suddenly in need of the smooth vanilla blend to calm her nerves.

"She can...transport herself. Hell, I don't even know the word for what she can do."

Lily scooped the pancakes off the griddle and set a plate in front of him. "We don't know for sure she did it. It could be some bizarre experiment of Reilly's."

"She did it in the cabin."

This was getting them nowhere. Lily scooped out two more spoonfuls of batter for herself with a jerky hand. "No. I haven't thought about professional help," she conceded. "I haven't even thought about how to decorate her bedroom."

"Well, word to the wise. Let her do that." He softened his tone and dug into the pancakes. "Little girls aren't always sugar and spice and everything nice," he said with a full mouth. On him it was cute. "Good flapjacks, by the way."

Lily ignored the trembling that had crept into her hands and forced a smile. She was thankful for his effort to lighten the situation. Every minute she spent with him she saw reasons his wife had fallen in love with him.

She ate quickly and then carried their dishes to the sink. "I'll be ready in a few minutes."

He stepped up behind her so quietly she sensed him before she heard him. He took a plate from her hand, making her nerve endings twitter. "I'll do these. You go do what you need to do."

Ordinarily it would have been a sweet gesture, but Lily sensed he wanted to be on his way as soon as possible.

She threw together a duffel bag with several pairs of jeans and shirts. Anticipating cold weather, she packed her winter jacket and a pair of gloves. Instead of trainers, she slipped into her hiking boots. If she encountered Colton Reilly's ogre again there would be no standing around like a fence post. She would give him a kick in the family jewels he wouldn't soon forget.

Miles was sitting on the couch tying his shoes with the cordless phone stuck against his shoulder when she came down.

"Okay. I'll tell her. We'll be leaving in about fifteen minutes. Yeah, thanks." He disconnected the call and set the handset on the table.

"Chief Billings?"

He fixed his pant leg and stood. She could tell by his expression the news was not good.

"They found more information on Luggo. He was a bounty hunter who had his license revoked in all three states they were issued in, including Washington. Whatever he's doing for Reilly is under the table. Billings put out a statewide APB on him this morning."

"Well, that's a relief." By his expression, she didn't think Miles agreed. "Isn't it?"

"We don't know how far-reaching his resources are. There's always a chance he's got more than one henchman and if he knows Luggo's been IDed, he might set someone else after you."

"Someone we don't recognize."

He nodded, his lips set in a firm line. "There's more."

Lily took a deep breath. "Should I sit down?" she asked, only half joking.

"The FBI has closed their investigation on IntelliGenysis."

Lily suddenly wished she hadn't eaten pancakes for breakfast. The sweet flavor of the syrup soured in her mouth. "Tell me something good."

A muscle in his jaw ticked. "I wish I could."

"That was a joke." She touched his elbow then bent to pick up her shoulder bag. "Are you ready to hit the road?"

"Lily, I think you should reconsider."

Halfway turned for the door, Lily stopped. That was the last straw. "You wouldn't sit on your hands if this was your child."

He froze, and Lily knew she'd hit a nerve.

"Because Annie isn't mine you think I shouldn't care as much? For God's sake, Miles."

He turned away and rubbed his face as if he was at his wit's end. "Jesus. I didn't say that."

"It's written all over your face. She's my niece. My last living family member. Five days ago I thought I had no one left, and then I was gifted with a miracle. Yes, I know it's dangerous, but I have to take whatever risks necessary to get her back. I hardly think asking questions of a woman who doesn't even work there anymore is life threatening."

Lily was trembling and her palms were damp. She turned and stormed for the door. "If you don't want to go with me, fine. Call the rental car agency. I'm sure they'd be happy to deliver another car."

She heard him on the carpet and a second later his hand touched her arm. "Lily."

She turned and gave her hardest stare, even though his gentle touch turned her insides to mush.

"The truth is I'm worried about you." His hand withdrew and he looked at the crook of her elbow where he'd touched her. "I don't want to see you hurt. You're no good to Annie dead."

She closed her eyes. *I don't want to see you hurt because I care about you* would have been better to hear.

"You have no obligation to me, Miles. You're not a police officer anymore."

"I might not wear a badge anymore, but I'll always be a cop," he said firmly. "At least let me help you. I know a thing or two about questioning people."

"You mean questioning people the *right* way."

He took her duffel bag as she opened the front door. "You

have to remember who this woman worked for."

"As if I could forget."

"She might keep silent out of loyalty to IntelliGenysis."

"Believe me, I'm going up there expecting the worst." She used the remote to unlock the doors and stopped to look at him over the car's roof. "Is she going to be questioned by a cop?"

"That's confidential police business." He winked. "Be thankful I'm willing to fudge the rules a little bit."

Lily opened the car door. "I don't want you to fudge the rules at all."

He grinned. "You can't get rid of me so easily."

Her stomach gave a tiny jump. "I'll just have to try harder next time."

Miles settled into the passenger seat. "I think we should stop at your bank before heading out of town. I'm not trying to tell you what to do, but you'd make me feel better if you used cash instead of credit when you're not in Seattle."

"I'm one step ahead of you. My assistant rented this car for me with her credit card."

"Smart thinking."

"Like you said, we have no idea how far reaching Colton's resources are."

When Lily emerged from the bank, what little sunshine had appeared that morning had been snuffed away by fast-spreading clouds. The first drops of rain hit the windshield as she turned onto interstate 90.

"I'm sorry," Lily said to break the silence. She didn't take her eyes from the road as he looked at her. "It was a horrible thing for me to say."

"I'm the one who should apologize." Miles sighed. "You were right. I would never sit still if it was Michelle who had been taken. I shouldn't have expected you would. It was just me being a cop again."

From the corner of her eye she saw him look out the window.

"It's frustrating to lose my chance with her," Lily risked in a whisper. "I just had a glimpse of her. I had only imagined what it would be like to have her in my life and then she was gone."

Miles sat up taller with a squeak of leather. "You'll get her back, Lily. I only hope you can be patient if it doesn't happen right away."

His voice came in a low timbre that resonated over every nerve ending. Not only was the man drop-dead sexy, but his voice was alluring and seductive as well. She imagined in the bedroom that voice couldn't be refused.

Unbidden and unwelcome, she pictured him with his wife. She had no idea what the woman had looked like, and in her thoughts there wasn't even a solid image, but the reverie brought a stab of something unfamiliar she was loathe to admit as jealousy. Simple things like afternoon walks and Sunday morning breakfasts with Miles must have been magical.

"I know Chief Billings meant well in advising me to hire a lawyer, but I feel the situation is more critical than that." She hesitated, choosing her words carefully. As lenient as he'd been with her so far, Miles was still a cop. "I believe Annie is in some kind of danger. Why else would my sister suddenly risk her life to get them out?"

A baited silence stretched as tightly as a freshly strung violin string.

When Miles spoke, his voice was low, almost regretful. "You know whatever happens I can't serve as a material witness for you. I'm no longer considered impartial where you're concerned."

The words were as clinical as they could possibly be, but they still warmed her insides. "Because we're friends?" she said, risking her hopes.

She glanced over and he smiled. "Because we're friends."

The rain grew more intense as they drove deeper into the mountains. By noon the sky was dark and heavy with rolling clouds and visibility was diminishing rapidly.

"Do you want me to drive for a while?"

"I'm fine," Lily lied. She was hungry and she had to pee.

"We should stop for lunch. I can hear your stomach grumbling."

"I prefer to keep going."

Miles adjusted himself in the seat. "Lily, don't worry. No one is following us."

Her stomach flip-flopped. The previous day's events were too horrific to consider again. "I want to get there as soon as possible."

"There's a small town up ahead with a decent Mexican restaurant. Do you like Mexican? I'm in the mood for some warm tortilla chips and salsa."

She laughed. "I see what you're trying to do."

"I'm not trying to do anything." He glanced out the window, smiling. "Refried beans and Spanish rice sound great right about now too."

Her stomach grumbled again. Her mouth watered for chips and salsa and refried beans with gooey, melted *queso fresco.* "All right, we'll stop."

Lily expected a greasy chain restaurant with mediocre food, but Mt. Pleasant Taqueria proved to be a friendly eatery with delicious homemade food and a comfortable, almost romantic ambiance. She and Miles were shown to a booth in the back corner of the restaurant which was filled mostly by blue collar workers on their lunch break. It was busy, but not noisy.

"Mexican food is a staple in all cops' diets," he said as he scooped a mountain of salsa onto a thick corn chip. "You've got to know the best place to get it."

"This seems a long way to go outside Seattle for Mexican food."

"We're only a half hour from Parkmont."

The romantic décor suddenly turned unwelcoming. Miles had probably taken his wife here. She looked down at her iced tea and stirred the lemon around with her straw.

Their server delivered steaming plates large enough to feed four people. Miles dug in like a starved man while Lily tried to decide what to eat and what to take in a to-go package.

"I'm thinking about reapplying to the force." He said it quietly, as if he suspected she was going to say, "You don't seem ready."

"I think that's a great idea." She took a bite of her chicken burrito and blew the steam into a napkin as it scalded her mouth.

"I have you to thank. I didn't realize how much I missed police work. And now that I've lost my garage, I have nothing else to do." He winked.

"Happy to be of service," she returned dryly.

Miles' smile faded. "The last three years have been hell, and I let myself wallow. I never should have quit the force, but for a while I was unfit to carry a badge. I'm ready to put it on again."

"You'll be a great cop." She knew it without a doubt. Miles had a powerfully honorable character. She felt lucky to call him friend, even luckier to have his help. "I've been thinking about Annie's appearances. She's never been to my townhouse. How do you think she knew where to appear?"

"I wondered about that too. I think she's tapped into us more than the physical location."

Lily nodded. That would make sense. She doubted Annie had ever been outside the compound before Cassie snuck her away.

A needling of worry had been eating away at her. What if her sister truly had stolen a child she had no right to? It wasn't like Cassie to keep quiet about something as significant as having a baby, yet she hadn't said a word at their last Christmas visit.

Lily had to accept the possibility she had no ties to Annie and no right to her.

But if that were true, why was Annie so connected to them she could visit them on a mental plane? Then again, Lily had to consider her abilities had nothing to do with biological ties. Annie had appeared to Miles, not to her, and they'd had no connection to him until they'd crashed into his station.

"Don't you think it's strange she appeared to you, not me?"

"Sweetheart, this whole thing is strange."

A wave of heat rushed from head to toe at his subtly placed endearment. "You seem so calm."

"Police training. Calm on the outside, no comment on the inside."

The waiter appeared and Lily waited while he cleared their plates.

"I almost feel selfish saying this, but I'm glad you saw her too. I might not believe any of this was real if I didn't have a witness. I'd probably be wearing a fitted jacket by now."

He issued a forlorn chuckle. "You're stronger than you give yourself credit for. More than I gave you credit for."

She held his gaze over the table. His eyes, now faded to the color of a pale Wyoming sky, bore into hers. His was a face she could look into forever.

The more time she spent with Miles the deeper she fell under his spell. His handsome good looks were enough to turn any woman's head, but there was much more to the attraction growing inside her. He was the most courageous man she'd ever known. He'd risked his life for her, dropped everything to help her.

Each minute spent with him magnified her appreciation a hundred fold. Each minute would make it harder to say goodbye. He'd already become much more than an acquaintance, much more than just a friend.

Her heart grew heavy as she realized they would probably part ways before the end of the day.

Chapter Twelve

It took almost three hours to reach Manning. Smoky black clouds made the afternoon seem more like evening and icy sheets of rain forced drivers to a crawl on the highway. Once they reached the quaint bedroom community, Miles guided Lily to Meiling Wong's home with the map she'd printed from the internet.

He'd been having second thoughts for the last hour, but he knew Lily couldn't be persuaded to abandon her plan. At best, he might convince her it would be a risk to his reinstatement, but then she would only insist on going without him.

She slowed the car on an impeccably maintained street where young cherry trees bent in the ferocious wind, desperately clinging to the last of their leaves.

"That's it, the one with the fountain." Water sprayed sideways from its two level tiers. All the tract homes looked the same, right down to the association-managed lawns and boxwood hedges. The only differences were small personal touches. He recognized the fountain in the center of Meiling's lawn, directly in front of the door, as Feng Shui decorating.

"Keep going," he said when she headed for the opposite curb.

"Why?" she asked, but swung the car away from the curb and continued down the street.

"You've never been on a stakeout, have you?"

Lily gave him a pursed smile that tickled his insides. "Of course not."

"Trust me on this. The house is dark. The first thing we need is food and coffee. We have no idea what time she'll be home. I want to see who comes and goes from the house before I go pounding on the door. The last thing I want is to have it answered by a husband who looks like a Sumo wrestler."

"All right, Officer Goodwin. You're the man in charge on this caper."

"I'd prefer if you didn't use the word 'caper'," he said wryly, making Lily laugh. The sound was pretty, and something jumped in that little place at the juncture of his ribs.

More laughter in his life would be a good thing, Miles realized. The melodious sound chased away the gloom seeping into the car from the bad weather outside, and a good chunk of the gloom tagging along with him the last three years of his life.

They left the residential area and found a strip mall with an Italian restaurant. Lily headed for the restroom while he ordered food to go and asked to see a local phone book. He flipped through the yellow pages and found several mid-range hotels nearby. With the weather worsening by the minute, he wasn't eager to spend any more time on the highway to Spokane than necessary.

Lily emerged as the waitress was ringing him up. "I'll pay," she said, nudging him aside. She picked up the bags and made a face at the weight. "I don't know what you ordered, but after the lunch we had, I won't be able to eat for two days."

"Trust me, you'll get hungry sitting in the car." He held his hand out for the keys. "I'll drive back."

Strong winds buffeted the Lincoln as they made their way back to Meiling Wong's house. Miles parked a few houses down and set his coffee cup on the dashboard. They sat in comfortable silence as the storm rattled the car. It might not be official, but being on a stakeout brought back pleasant memories and convinced him his choice to reapply was the right one.

"After your sister was struck by lightning, did she have any physical injuries?" he asked Lily.

"Do you mean something that would indicate why she changed?" Lily shifted toward him and brought one leg onto the seat. "Only burns to her hands and thighs where she was in contact with the ground. She was kept in the hospital for two days to monitor some irregularity in her heartbeat, but that was merely a cautionary standard."

Lily looked past him at the empty house. Her eyes took on a far-away wistfulness. "My mother and I were more worried about her emotional state. She took her boyfriend's death hard. A psychiatrist told us she had survivor's guilt."

"How long after the lightning strike did she become convinced she could hear other people's thoughts?"

Lily took a deep breath as she thought about it. "I'm not exactly sure. She acted differently from the moment she came home." Her mouth quirked downward. "We didn't know what to do. We probably assumed all the wrong things, but she wouldn't talk to us. We had no idea how to deal with her problems."

Lily flipped a lock of hair back from her face. "She wasn't being any more difficult than a typical girl her age, but that was the thing, Cassie had been such an all-American girl before. She had been popular, smart, absolutely beautiful. She liked frilly things. She was a varsity-squad cheerleader. She dramatically changed her appearance and not for the better. She became sullen and bitchy all the time. She was so difficult it was easier for us to ignore her than to try and communicate with her."

"What you describe sounds like the experiences of families of drug addicts," Miles said cautiously. "The person's sudden change in behavior shocks the family, making them withdraw."

"If only it were drugs." She pulled a piece of thread from the seam of her jeans and twisted it between two fingers. "I was only fifteen. I didn't know any better. There are a million things I wish I'd done differently, but it's useless to dwell on it now."

Miles sighed. Truer words were never spoken.

"Cassandra finished her senior year of high school at home." Lily went on. "She'd been an honor student and earned a scholarship to Berkeley. There's a special classification for students who suffer life-altering injury before going to college, so she didn't lose her scholarship."

"Lucky for her," Miles interjected.

"I guess it was over the summer we first noticed the depth of the changes in her. Each year there was a picnic at the park our community surrounded. Cassie and I were arguing about a neighbor's recipe for brownies. She claimed the woman lied about her ingredients—she had to be using lard even though she said she hadn't. Finally, Cassie said she knew the woman lied because she could read her thoughts. I told my mother and of course she questioned Cassie about it. She acted like it was no big deal. As casually as if she were saying she wanted steak for dinner, she told my mother ever since the strike she could hear other people's thoughts. I thought Cassie was just being...Cassie."

Lily gave him a secret look and smiled. Miles felt an unexpected lurch all the way into his toes. She had a dimple in her right cheek which only came out occasionally.

"She looked at us and said we were thinking she was crazy.

135

Well, of course that was what we were thinking."

Miles laughed and then realized it was inconsiderate. "Sorry."

But Lily only shook her head and gazed out the window, smiling. "Don't be. I know how crazy it must make her sound." She took a deep breath and let out a long sigh. "Only now, after what I've seen, I know she wasn't crazy at all."

She turned back with complete seriousness in those fathomless brown eyes. "It had to be real. How else could she have given birth to such a gifted child?"

Gifted wasn't the word Miles would have used. He wasn't sure what word was the best to describe Annie, but he did know the little girl's abilities made him shiver.

He placed his hand over Lily's where it rested on her thigh. Immediately, he knew it was a mistake, but it was too late to move it without seeming odd. "Lily, you need to consider—" He broke off when he remembered how angry she'd become at Chief Billings' suggestion the day before, not sure how to put it without angering her all over again.

"That Annie wasn't really her daughter?" Lily clearly knew exactly what he meant. She glanced out the windshield as leaves blew past the car. "I have. But I was also thinking about how much she looks like Cassandra did at her age. Actually, she looks even more like my mother."

Miles drew his hand away. The warmth of Lily's skin slowly faded from his fingertips.

She looked down at her hand where he'd touched her. The forlorn reservation covering her features proved she had picked up on his aversion to physical contact.

Her gaze rose to his and a tiny smile touched her lips. It faded immediately. His heart hardened as he realized she might be attracted to him. He had nothing to give her.

136

He could never act on his physical needs for Lily. There could never be another woman for him. It was wrong to even have these feelings.

He glanced out the window as silence settled over them again. Slowly, neighbors began arriving home. The bad weather proved a good cover. Thanks to the thick, black clouds it was already dark. People hurried inside and no one came out to mow the lawns in the sideways rain. At seven-thirty the light by Meiling's front door and the walkway lights clicked on at the same time.

"How are you doing? Do you want to take a break?"

Lily shook her head. "I'm fine."

A silver Mercedes pulled into the drive. She clutched Miles' arm. "She's home."

"Someone's home," he corrected her.

The garage door opened to an empty garage with a washer and dryer by the door leading into the house, but little else. A stack of cardboard boxes was piled against the left wall. No set of family bicycles, no toys, no tools.

"She parked in the middle. Let's go." Before he could stop her, Lily had the door open and one foot on the sidewalk.

He jumped out from the driver's side and followed her across the street. Too late he realized he should have been instructing her on the proper etiquette of questioning instead of memorizing the pretty nuances of her face. Lily was desperate and liable to make a mess of things.

The temperature had dropped significantly in the last two hours, but he expected Lily's speed as she headed for Meiling's door was from excitement, not because of the rain. He grabbed her arm to slow her as they hit the path. "Let me do the talking," he managed to say before she pushed the doorbell.

An attractive Asian woman pulled back the curtain on the narrow window beside the door. "Who is there?" she called through the glass.

Miles showed his badge. "Miles Goodwin, Seattle Police."

He found himself under Lily's questioning gaze, but she didn't comment.

"Tiny fib," he whispered.

The woman disappeared from the window and a moment later the door cracked open. "Is there a problem?"

"Ms. Wong, we'd like to ask some questions about your time at IntelliGenysis."

She frowned. "I've already spoken to the Spokane police and the FBI. I can't tell you anything more, and frankly I wish you would stop bothering me."

The door started to close. Lily shoved it open.

Ms. Wong staggered back a step with a look of utter disbelief on her face as Lily stalked inside.

"You have no right!"

Yep, he should have been giving her some pointers. The questioning had gone to hell in under a minute. A new record for him.

"Ms. Wong, he's with the police, I'm not. You can either answer my questions willingly, or I'll force them out of you."

Shit.

The terrified woman glanced from Lily to him. He stepped inside but held the door open. "Lily."

Meiling threw a bitter scowl at her. "I will tell you the same thing I told the others. I signed a proprietary agreement. I cannot talk to you without a warrant."

Lily's body language revealed defeat, but clearly she wasn't ready to give up yet. "I'm not here in an official capacity. My name is Lily Brent. Cassandra Brent was my sister."

"Was?"

"She's dead. She was murdered trying to get her daughter away from the facility. Annie Brent, did you know her?"

"You mean A2-6."

Lily tossed a wide-eyed gaze at Miles.

"Yes, I knew her."

She held up a tiny hand. Meiling's fingers were slender and delicate, but the pinky finger was twisted and bent, as if it had been broken so badly it couldn't be properly fixed.

"Leave her there. The child is dangerous. Take my word for it."

Chapter Thirteen

Lily was afraid if she didn't sit down she would fall down.

"Did Annie do that to you?"

Silence ticked out like a too-slow clock. "No." Meiling finally said, but her severe expression didn't change. "Don't go to IntelliGenysis. Nothing good will come of it."

"Why did you call her A2-6?"

"Because it's her name."

Miles moved up behind Lily and placed a hand at the small of her back. Not only did she feel like she was going to fall over, she must have looked it.

"Ms. Wong, a week ago a counselor from the Spokane Department of Child Protective Services told me I was the guardian of a child I didn't even know my sister had. She turned over a frightened little girl who has never played with a puppy or watched *Sesame Street*. That's all I know about her. Then she was taken from me at gunpoint by a man the size of a linebacker. I'm going to get her back if it's the last thing I do."

"It very well may be."

"Please, Ms. Wong. I need your help. You're the only one who can answer questions which may mean the difference between success and failure. I need to understand what's going on at IntelliGenysis."

Meiling glanced away as she chewed her lip. Lily held her breath. With a sigh, the woman turned and sat in a love seat. Hoping that was an invitation, Lily perched opposite her on the couch. Miles closed the door and sat beside her.

The woman wrung her hands together, and when she spoke her delicate voice was hardly more than a whisper. "I know the man you're talking about. I'm surprised you're still alive." She took a deep, shuddering breath. "My talking to you could get me killed."

"I won't reveal anything you say to us," Lily promised. "Please, Ms. Wong."

Meiling closed her eyes over a long heartbeat. Lily gripped the thick couch cushion, silently pleading.

The woman opened her eyes. Her expression now seemed resigned. "What do you want to know?"

"Why is Annie so valuable to Colton Reilly?" Miles asked her.

"She's his most successful subject," Meiling answered simply. "Or she was at the time of my resignation a year ago."

"What are they doing to her?" Lily was almost afraid of the answer, but she had to know.

"Annie is part of an experiment called Project Midnight."

She glanced at Miles. His stony expression revealed nothing.

"My sister claimed to have psychic abilities. Does this have something to do with this project?"

"It has everything to do with it." Meiling settled back onto the love seat as if reluctant, but also relieved a long journey was ending in her decision to talk. "One doesn't apply to IntelliGenysis—one is recruited. Colton Reilly hired me before he restricted himself to hiring only those with paranormal abilities, or belief in the paranormal." She grimaced. "I should rephrase that as *fanatical* belief. I had always believed on a scientific level the human brain possesses vast powers unknown, but I wasn't obsessive about it. Colton hired me because of my breakthroughs with cures in inherited birth defects through the use of gene splicing."

"Your drug RH24," Lily supplied.

"Yes. But I wanted to work on diseases. Colton focused all his work in two divisions, advanced intelligence and psychic abilities."

A piece of the puzzle clicked into place. "What kind of psychic abilities?"

"Telekinetics—telekinesis, telepathy, teleportation."

Teleportation. She glanced at Miles. His gaze flicked from her back to Meiling.

"What was he doing to Annie?"

"Annie." She gave a humorless chuckle and shook her head. "Annie was the most remarkable breakthrough in his studies. She's more advanced than any adult I've seen. The last I saw her she was about to turn five, but already more powerful than children twice her age in the telekinetics division.

"But Annie is rebellious. It was a phenomenon we witnessed in some children, but again, stronger in Annie. Though she had no way of knowing because she'd never been taught as much, she believed it was wrong to do the things we asked of her." Her gaze fell. "It's just more evidence of Annie's advanced intelligence. Unlike other children, she possesses the ability to gauge her actions as right or wrong. The boy who did this to me," Meiling held up her hand, "also knew the difference, but he chose to do wrong. Those children are dangerous. They lack the maturity to make coherent decisions about their behavior."

"You just said she was more advanced than adults," Miles interjected. He looked shell shocked. Lily's heart went out to him. It was horrific to imagine someone treating a child as nothing more than a laboratory specimen.

"More advanced—yes. More mature? No. Children have fantastic imaginations, they throw temper tantrums, they're upset by trivial things. There are chemical reasons why children behave differently than adults and these chemicals are what make children with special abilities dangerous."

"Surely you don't believe Annie is dangerous?" Lily pressed.

Meiling looked at her like she was dumb. "You don't understand. He's building an army. Why do you think the FBI investigation was dropped? The United States government is one of his most optimistic customers."

"Then why an investigation in the first place?" Lily wondered aloud.

Meiling gave a disinterested shrug. "Propaganda. To keep an eye on their investment. Maybe just making sure Colton knew they were in charge. You tell me."

"It sounds like you're saying he's creating little monsters." Miles' voice was low with disgust. Lily took his hand and held it in both of hers.

"The projects are more sophisticated than that, but Colton Reilly is insane. He believes his experiments will pave the way for an advanced race of people with psychic abilities. That in the future there will be two types of people—those with psychic abilities, and those without."

"What kind of things do they make her do?" Lily asked. Her heart twisted for Annie. Six years old was too young to comprehend the atrocities of mankind.

"The studies are quite mundane. Moving blocks around on a table, solving puzzles without touching them, reading the

143

contents on the backs of cards. It is all very typical of psychic testing, only at IntelliGenysis it isn't fun like what you see on television. It's the real deal. Frighteningly real."

"Where does gene splicing come in?" Miles asked.

"To factor in psychic abilities, of course. This is why he seeks people who exhibit or have experienced psychic phenomena to work for him."

"Like my sister."

Meiling nodded, grave acknowledgement in her eyes. "Like your sister." She looked back at Miles. "This was my arena. I was responsible for the studies identifying and isolating the genes making these people different."

It was all racing around in Lily's head much too fast. It was like the Superman syndrome. On earth, Superman was truly super, but on Krypton he was just like everyone else. What good would psychic abilities be if everyone had them?

"He's building wax wings," Lily spat. "He's a fool."

"There is a fine line between genius and insanity," Meiling reminded her. "Imagine having a spy who could eavesdrop on a conversation in another room simply with the power of his mind? A judge who can read the mind of a killer on trial? A soldier who can control weapons from a distance—control *anything* from a distance?" She snorted. "I'm in no way condoning it, but his theory is like a weapon of mass destruction. It's a horrible thing, but you can't help but be in awe of it. Now do you see why the government wants their stake?"

That was a scary thought she didn't want to contemplate. When she'd believed the FBI was investigating IntelliGenysis, she saw them as an ally. But now that she knew they wanted Colton Reilly to build them psychic soldiers, Lily felt alone and insignificant against a gigantic and powerful enemy.

"Annie is afraid of the dark. She said they make her sleep in the water. What does that mean? When she appeared to us, she was all wet."

Meiling's eyes grew wide. "She appeared to you?"

"Twice," Lily told her. "Rather, to Miles."

Meiling stood and paced around her couch. "I always knew she was different from the rest, but I had no idea." It seemed she spoke more to herself than to them.

"Annie said she had nineteen brothers and sisters. Are these all children of the employees?"

She gave that sardonic laugh again, as though Lily was as naive as a child. "They are all *his* children. Each and every one is his offspring. He believes he is responsible for their superior genetic traits."

"Dear God," Miles breathed out. "He really is crazy."

"That's why he's not married to any of the women and hasn't legally adopted Annie." Lily surmised out loud. "He couldn't possibly get away with adopting nineteen children without raising questions of ethics." How could her smart, vivacious sister have fallen prey to this man?

"There were twenty children in Project Midnight alone."

Lily gaped at her, speechless.

"There are other projects," Meiling confirmed. She returned to her seat across from them. "There were fifty-two children in all. Six died during my time at IntelliGenysis."

"From what?" Miles demanded gruffly. Lily squeezed his hand.

"Illnesses attributed to their studies. Drug overdoses. Colton is desperate for results; he pushes them too hard. Shortly before I left, Colton ordered a scientist named Alexandrov to introduce drugs into a group of subjects performing at a slower rate than the others, hoping to bring them up to speed."

Her sentence hung in the air, unfinished. She stared at the floor for a long moment. When she lifted her gaze, it was filled with guilt. "There was a little boy like Annie, stronger and more advanced than the others. Only four years old. His heart simply stopped."

Miles winced.

"How horrible," Lily breathed out.

"One of the mothers walked out with her child and took hold of the electric fence. The child died but the mother survived. Then she disappeared. No one asked where...that's one of the reasons the FBI launched their investigation."

"Why did you leave?" Lily asked her.

Meiling tried to appear subtle as she dabbed at the corner of her eye, but Lily could see the first moisture of new tears shining there. "I told you, I want to cure diseases, not cause them. I wanted no part of his evil."

"Six children have died because of his greed." Miles closed his eyes. "Jesus."

"What does the water mean?" Lily pressed.

"The children are isolated in sensory deprivation chambers. The study is named Project Midnight because the subjects exhibit their strongest abilities in REM sleep when totally removed from external stimuli."

A chill rolled over Lily. "That must be why Annie is afraid of the dark."

"It is scary for her, but Annie isn't in any danger." Meiling pursed her lips. "It's the people on the outside who are at risk."

"Unless they start pumping her with drugs," Lily shot back.

"The drugs are only used on the weaker subjects who don't

advance at the same rate as the others."

That was little consolation. Colton was insane. What if he punished Annie for running? It wasn't even her fault, but Lily didn't expect him to be capable of pity.

"What kind of drugs is he using?" Miles growled the question through clenched teeth.

Lily was starting to worry about him. He'd hardly been able to tolerate Annie's presence. She could tell by his graying pallor and trembling hand that Meiling's stories were pushing him over the edge. These were horrendous crimes against children.

Meiling shook her head. "I don't know exactly. At first it was just adrenaline fed through an intravenous line, but then he started using Ketamine. It's used medically for sedation, though in some people it can induce hallucinations. That was enough to make me resign. I told you, I haven't been there in over a year. I can't say what he's done recently to make your sister want to escape."

Escape. The word caused Lily to shudder. The idea her sister had been the captive of a maniacal monster made her sick to her stomach.

"Leaving wasn't easy," Meiling said on a soft breath. "I look over my shoulder every day."

"No one will ever know we were here," Lily assured her. "I promise you, we won't reveal your name or anything you've told us to anyone."

"What can you tell us about security?" Miles asked Meiling.

Was he considering going inside with her? More likely, he was building his argument to convince her not to try, but Lily was more convinced than ever she had to.

"They don't call it a compound for nothing," Meiling returned. "The entire facility is surrounded by electrified fence, including the living quarters."

Lily shuddered. Annie's spectral warning haunted her. *Don't touch the fences.*

"There are sixty cottages on the property, just like a military base. His closest employees live in luxury apartments in the main building. Lower-ranking employees who don't have access to confidential information leave and return on a daily basis."

She hadn't expected this. "How do they get in and out?"

"People travel freely in and out through a guard station at the main entrance. When I worked there, security was outsourced through Adeptco."

Lily frowned. "If they can come and go, what makes them return?"

"Golden handcuffs. Fear tactics. It's different for everyone. Those without scruples get paid to stay. Those with a conscience are scared within an inch of their sanity. You see your good friend try to resign and then he disappears, or has an accident, and you're sure not going to risk that."

"How did you manage to get out?" Lily asked, barely able to conceal her anger. Why was this woman allowed to leave with her life when her sister was killed like nothing more than an annoying insect?

"I'm too well known. I was nominated for the Pulitzer." She glanced down. "Maybe it was because I got out that your sister tried too."

"How do you know Vince Luggo?" Miles asked. Meiling returned a confused stare. "He's the man who attacked us."

"Ah. He follows Colton around like a lap dog." She shook her head. "He doesn't talk to anybody. I didn't know his name."

"Are there others like him?"

"No other bodyguard types, I think, but he's got plenty of lackeys to do his dirty work." She shrugged. "Over the past year, anything could have changed."

"What about security inside?" he pressed. "Annie told us there were no cameras on the roof."

"I've never been on the roof. I couldn't say if she's right or not. But if Annie is teleporting herself, there's no telling what she's seen. I would bet she's right." Meiling nodded. "That's where the helipad is located, and Colton is very secretive about his comings and goings. It would make sense he doesn't want cameras there."

"Do you know how many security officers there are?" Lily asked her.

"There are usually only two guards on duty at a time, one guard at the gate, and one in the control room, because everything that happens is recorded on video tape." She pursed her lips in a smirk. "Of course, that's to protect him and him alone. Security isn't an issue on the inside. Employees can only travel as far as they're allowed by electronic pass codes."

Lily's hope spiked. "What was your pass code?"

"Deleted when I took my exit interview." Meiling frowned. "I know what you're planning, but I can't help you. It will be impossible for you to get inside." She sighed, shaking her head, as if she knew Lily would try anyway.

There was nothing the other woman could say to convince her away now. Lily was getting Annie out of there, one way or another.

"People have disappeared from IntelliGenysis. If you truly intend to go in there, be careful. Colton won't be very forgiving toward anyone who tries to interfere with his master plan."

Chapter Fourteen

The wind had slacked off, leaving fat, icy raindrops to fall straight to the ground.

Once outside on Meiling's driveway, Lily's composure fell. She covered her face with her hands and Miles heard the gasp that would lead to sobs. He took her under his arm and brought her close.

"Let's get out of the rain."

He glanced back. Meiling peered out of the narrow window beside the door. Her gaze slipped away, her eyes full of regret, and she let the sheer curtain drift back into place.

Nothing that happened at IntelliGenysis was the woman's fault, but he was glad she felt guilty. She wouldn't have given them information if she didn't.

He guided Lily to the passenger side and helped her in, then hurried to the driver's side. He started the car. The windshield wipers thumped back and forth, a dreary sound on a bleak night. Meiling had given them nothing but hopelessness.

But Lily wasn't convinced. He knew her well enough already to understand she was stronger than that.

"It's worse than I thought," Lily said quietly. She stared straight forward at nothing, her eyes unfocussed. "He's using her for evil."

"You heard Ms. Wong. Annie knows the difference between right and wrong better than most adults."

A silver tear rolled down Lily's cheek. "She's so scared, all by herself there." She turned to him. "It's different, now. Before, she had Cassandra. Now she's all alone."

"We're going to get her out." He grasped her hand where it rested on her thigh. It was wet from the rain and ice cold. "Even if we can't get inside, we can make such a public spectacle he'll give her up to quiet the scandal."

Lily shook her head and her composure fell. "He'll never willingly give her up. You heard her, Annie is his most successful experiment."

He gave her hand a squeeze. "We'll figure a way."

Miles put the car in drive and drove out of the residential area. They'd come in on Hastings, which was the main street in town. One of the hotel ads in the phone book had a cursory map directing travelers off Hastings.

"Where are we going?" Lily asked when he didn't drive to the highway.

"Command central." Up ahead he saw the sign for the Holiday Inn. The neighborhood didn't seem too bad and the hotel appeared modern and well maintained. He turned into the parking lot and parked in the front by registration. "It's almost nine and we're both tired."

Miles shut off the engine and turned to Lily. "You didn't plan to drive up to IntelliGenysis and bang on the door, did you? You need to absorb what you just learned and formulate a plan."

She looked like she wanted to protest, and he couldn't help but admire her for it.

"My head is spinning with what I just learned and I know yours is too," he told her. "Trust me, you need to reassemble yourself before you make any hasty decisions."

To his surprise, she quirked a smile. "Is this Officer Goodwin speaking?"

"Actually it's Lieutenant First Class Goodwin. I served in the Marines."

Lily laughed. "Now why didn't I guess that?" She grabbed her purse and hurried with him through the rain.

A young woman greeted them with a smile. "Do you have a reservation?"

Miles shook his head. "I saw your vacancy sign and thought I'd take a gamble."

She clicked on her computer. "The bad weather brought you in off the highway, did it? Good choice. I heard on the radio a jackknifed big rig shut the down highway two miles north of here. I have a single king with a mini-kitchen available, non smoking."

His empty stomach clenched. "We'll need two rooms."

"I'm sorry, sir. It's our only room available, and that's only because of a last minute cancellation."

Lily glanced at him uneasily and Miles began to sweat. "Can you call a nearby hotel and see if there are any other rooms available?"

The young lady smiled. "I'll be glad to, sir, but there's a cheerleading rally in town this week. We've been sold out for months."

"That's okay," Lily said. "I'm sure the room is fine. Will it be all right if I pay cash?"

The woman's gaze slid to Lily, no longer smiling. "Yes, but I'll need to see some ID and you'll be required to put down a sixty dollar deposit per night in addition to the room charges. Fully refundable, of course."

Miles opened his badge. "How's this?"

"Oh." Rebecca, her name tag read, relaxed and her smile returned. "Fine. Thank you, officer." She clicked on her keyboard again. "And I'll be happy to waive the deposit. The rally ends tomorrow and many of our guests will be checking out in the morning. I'm sure I'll be able to find a second room for you for tomorrow night."

Miles resisted the urge to say that would be a hundred years too late.

She handed Lily the key. "Your room is upstairs and on the left side. There's a stairway at the center and end of the wing. We serve a continental breakfast from six until nine in the lounge behind the lobby, and there's a coffee maker in your room."

"Thank you, Rebecca," Lily said.

Miles followed Lily outside. She didn't say anything as they returned to the car and drove to the far end of the hotel wing. Sure enough, the parking lot was filled with mini-vans emblazoned with high school slogans in bright, temporary paint.

He took her bag and followed Lily up the stairs. She unlocked the room and moved inside, setting her purse on the table.

Miles stood in the doorway on feet refusing to move inside. The single, king-size bed stood in the center of the room like a sacrificial dais. A lump formed in his throat. He drew a deep breath and forced his feet to step into the room. The bed seemed to grow larger in his peripheral vision.

He dropped Lily's duffel bag on the chair beside the table. "I think I should head home. I live about an hour and a half away.

153

I can come back for you in the morning."

Lily stopped rifling through her purse. She looked up with that deer-in-headlights expression. "Don't be ridiculous." As if reading his mind, she turned and looked at the bed. "Miles, this isn't a big deal. We're both adults, we can make this work."

Her voice shook as she said it. She was as uncomfortable as he was. He searched for an excuse. None came as a long minute ticked by. A gust of wind blew in and crept through his clothes like icy fingers. He turned and closed the door.

Lily abandoned whatever she was looking for and stepped closer.

"You've already done so much for Annie and me, and I don't have the right to ask anything more of you." She swallowed. "But I don't want to be alone tonight. Please, stay."

He looked down at the carpeting, unable to face the desolation in her eyes.

"I know these past few days have been especially hard for you, and I respect what you're going through. I would never do anything.... I would never intentionally make it worse for you."

She smiled and touched his forearm in a tender, yet entirely platonic gesture. His appreciation for her doubled.

"Maybe we can call up for an extra cot."

He forced a laugh. It sounded brittle. "No, you're right. We're not teenagers."

Miles did his best to straighten his shoulders. As difficult as it was to be frank, he wanted no misinterpretation. "It's just that I've slept alone since..." He turned away and drove his fingers through his hair. "You're right. It has been hard to be with you and Annie. You've made me remember things I thought were gone for good."

When he faced her again, Lily looked solemn. He wished he

had more to give her. She deserved so much more.

"Things I wasn't ready to remember." He grimaced. "You could say it was a crash course."

A slow smile touched her lips. He smiled too. Some of the tension drained out of him.

"I appreciate that you've been sensitive," he finished.

"I wouldn't be a very good friend if I wasn't." She turned back to her purse and found the bottle of aspirin she'd been looking for. "I'm hungry after all. I'm going to stick one of these pasta containers in the microwave."

"Stick them both in. I'm starved too." He gave her a sly look. "I told you I knew how to manage a stakeout."

"I'll never doubt you again," she said.

He wondered if she would hold true to that tomorrow morning when it came time to finalize their plan.

Lily hand washed some silverware and set it aside on paper towels. Though she had no doubt the dishwasher worked fine and there was probably a maid who did the final cleaning after each guest, she felt better doing them herself and *knowing* they were clean.

She set out two steaming plates of Fettuccini Alfredo on the guest table and poured them each a glass of water.

"I've been thinking about how to approach IntelliGenysis," she said lightly as she folded paper towels to use as napkins and set out the cleaned silverware. She broke the loaf of French bread at the middle and set half on each plate. She waited until she knew Miles wasn't going to respond before going on, certain he was poised to voice argument against both her ideas.

She sat and dug into the pasta, savoring the creamy sauce. "Mmm. Italian is always better after it's rested a while."

Miles eyed her.

"Okay, so I was thinking." She wiped her mouth with a napkin as he folded his arms over his chest. One brow twitched upward.

"Idea one. We go up there and demand a meeting. See what kind of game plan he has."

"That could be disastrous. He tried to kill us, remember? I'm not about to willingly jump into that spider's web."

"I didn't say these were good ideas," she returned. He would like the next idea even less. She dug back into the pasta, mustering up her courage. "But Vince Luggo didn't try to shoot me. He intentionally aimed above my head at the rest stop."

"True or not, storming up to the door puts you at a severe disadvantage. He could do whatever he wanted to you and no one would ever know. You heard Meiling; people have disappeared from there."

"Idea two. Meiling also said the security department is outsourced. Well, if there are executive apartments inside the main building, there has to be a maid service, right? I'll bet that's outsourced too. If we could find out what company they use, maybe I could get a job as a maid. I can get my office to provide a fake job reference for me—"

Miles had been shaking his head back and forth the entire time. "Bad idea," he said. "I don't like the thought of you sneaking in there. Besides, it wouldn't work. He knows what you look like."

"Does he keep a personal eye on his maids?" she countered.

"Who the hell knows?" Miles continued shaking his head. "It wouldn't work."

"What do you propose?"

"I need to think on it. Let me ask you this, what are you going to do when you get Annie back?"

Some of her tension evaporated. She liked the fact he'd said *when*, not *if*.

"Well, I had an idea for that too, but now that I think about it, I've changed my mind."

He gave her a skeptical look. "You're not even going to run it by me?"

"You don't seem to like my ideas much."

"Give me a shot." He grinned. "I promise I won't shoot it down. Not immediately, anyway."

"I'll shoot it down myself. It's too dangerous." She looked down at her plate and twirled pasta around her fork. "No."

"All right," he said, waiting until she'd finished chewing. "At least tell me what it was."

"I was thinking Annie and I could fly to New York. I have a good friend there. My assistant could buy the tickets out of Spokane. But first I will have used my credit card to rent a car that someone..."

"Me."

"...drives in the other direction."

"What's wrong with that plan?"

"The last time someone switched places with me, she ended up dead."

He opened his mouth but she didn't give him the chance to speak.

"It's too dangerous. Even if you are a cop *and* a marine. I won't let you do it."

"Colton Reilly knows who I am. Chances are if Annie goes missing he'll come looking at my house. No matter where I am,

I'm going to have to keep my guard up and my head down."

Lily set her fork down. "God." A hot wave of guilt rushed through her midsection. Her appetite vanished. "I'm so sorry."

"Lily." Miles reached across the small table and grasped her hand. In his tight grip she could feel his strength and courage. That only made it harder to swallow the whole wretched mess.

"None of this is your fault. We're both victims. All three of us. The only one to blame is Colton."

Her throat tightened with sorrow. She stared at his hand and then, with resignation, brought her gaze up to his. "Would I be a horrible person if I don't say I wish I'd never met you?"

He smiled as he leaned back against the chair. "Would I be a lunatic if I don't say I wish you hadn't either?"

She choked out a laugh over the sob struggling to break free.

"The way I see it we need two plans. The first one to get Annie out of IntelliGenysis, the second to get you both out of Dodge. Once we get her there won't be a lot of time to figure out plan two."

"You're right. If I don't act fast, I'll be right back where I started."

Leaving the state meant leaving Miles. She'd known as much, had even expected he would be gone by now. But somehow, planning an out-of-state flight cemented the idea.

Lily pushed the thought out of her mind. She didn't want to consider never seeing him again.

Her whole life she had existed in pursuit of long-term goals. Everything she did was part of a plan for the future. It was time to live in the moment, and this moment was spent with Miles. *Don't think about later, when he'll be gone.*

"I like the part about leaving the state, but I think Reilly will anticipate the airport," he said. "We should consider alternatives."

"Like what?"

"Maybe finding you a place to hide out in Spokane for a while."

Her heart thumped against her ribs. Was he going to suggest living with him?

"If Reilly thinks you're on the run he's going to spread out looking for you. If you lay low he'll look right past you."

She opened her mouth but nothing came out besides an awkward "bwa" sound.

"Eddie has a house in Spokane. His wife passed away about ten years ago. I'm sure he'd let you stay with him for as long as you need. Eddie would love to play cop again."

"Are you sure you'd want to ask him? Anyone I'm near would be in danger." Which still meant she couldn't see Miles, even if she was only ten minutes away.

Lily rose and took their empty plates to the kitchen. "I don't think you should ask him. I'm sure in his heart he'd love to help, but he's not up to it. It wouldn't be fair to ask."

"I can't arrange for you to be placed in a safe house. What I'm doing isn't exactly on the record."

"I know." She rinsed the plates and opened the dishwasher. "I think I should stick to the airport plan. Maybe I could buy a wig for myself and a hat for Annie. You know, without an airline ticket, Colton and his goon can't get through airport security."

"What's to stop him from buying a cheap ticket somewhere?" Miles countered. "He wouldn't blink at the cost."

She sighed, defeated. "I still think it's the best idea." She resigned herself to the fact he wasn't going to like it.

Was it too much to hope he didn't want her to leave, either?

Lily dropped their dishes into the dishwasher. She closed it and faced him. "I'm going to take a shower. If you think up a better plan, let me know."

Lily emerged from the bathroom about forty-five minutes later. Her hair was messy but dry, as if she'd wound it up in a towel. She wore powder blue, satiny pajamas with ivory piping. The pants and long-sleeved shirt covered everything but her hands and feet.

Miles pretended to turn his attention back to the news and bit back a smile. The threadbare t-shirt he'd caught her in the night before had been an accident. She was probably embarrassed about it, but he would bet for the wrong reason. Sure, it had a ragged, too-short hem and been so thin it left little to the imagination, but she probably didn't realize it had been outrageously sexy. In his mind's eye he could still see the tight peaks of her nipples and dark circles of her areolas. In fact, he couldn't get them *out* of his mind's eye.

"Did you leave me any hot water?" he asked as he shifted on the chair. Suddenly, his jeans felt too tight.

"Probably not." Lily gingerly peeled back the top corner of the bedcovers, as if she would sleep on the very edge of the left side. He smothered another grin. Her shyness was another trait he adored about her.

An uncomfortable lump formed in his throat. He was letting his thoughts run away with him, in the *wrong* direction.

It seemed like forever since he'd enjoyed the company of a woman, even thought about sharing intimacy. He'd believed that part of his life had died with Sara. He'd watched Eddie live alone for ten years after Claire died and thought he would be no different. Most cops he knew were either unmarried or divorced. His choice had not been a hard one.

But now he ached from the desire Lily stirred in him. She was beautiful, sweet, caring, modest and sexy as hell. Resisting the feelings she brought to life took Herculean strength, and he just didn't have it anymore.

Miles realized the news had ended and a late night drama filled the screen. He flipped the television off. Silence bounced off the walls.

He would never act on his feelings, but that wasn't what was bothering him. It was the feelings themselves, invading a part of himself he wanted kept empty. Untouched. The part of himself that had been content with loneliness and darkness.

Now he reached toward the light she'd brought into his life like a drowning man swimming toward rays of sun visible at the surface of a deep sea.

"There are three pillows. Do you mind if I have the extra?" Her timid voice stirred up those feelings all over again like a breeze touching a pile of leaves.

"There are four pillows."

She held one up. "This one's a potato chip."

He shrugged. "I don't mind."

Lily sat on the bed and pulled the covers over herself, confirming his suspicions she would sleep as far away from him as she was capable. He admired her for the effort as much as she amused him by it. Sweet Lily.

"Was there anything on the news?"

He shook his head, knowing she meant *anything related to IntelliGenysis.* "I'm going to take a quick shower."

If there was no hot water left, all the better. He closed the door and pressed his head against the cool wood. There was indeed a jackknifed big rig stopping traffic in both directions on Highway 395, but Miles suspected he would be better off sitting in the car on a dark highway than sharing a bed with Lily.

Her toothbrush stood upright in a glass, and she'd left him a brand new one, still in its package, on the counter by the sink. He was doomed.

There was plenty of hot water. He let it sting his skin. It only made the hot desire pulsing through his body grow worse. He turned the water to cold, but that didn't help either. He emerged, brushed his teeth and then used the hair dryer Lily had left in her travel bag on the counter. Finally, there was nothing more he could do to delay going back out there. He slipped into his jeans and opened the door.

Lily lay sideways on her elbow and two pillows, flipping channels. It was after eleven and the prime channels were now running a recap of national news.

"I was wrong. All these pillows are potato chips." She hit the off button and the room went dark except for the light spilling out of the bathroom door.

"You want me to call the desk?" He flipped the light off, unable to look at her in that silky blue material that beckoned to his hands.

No, it's not the material, but the curves beneath.

"I'll be fine. I'll probably snore, though."

He chuckled. He appreciated her efforts to lighten the tension that was probably written across his face.

But turning the light off was a mistake. Now there was only the patter of rain outside and the silvery light seeping through too-sheer curtains.

"Um, I was thinking," he started awkwardly. He stepped into the room and rounded the bed to the far side. "If Annie appears, maybe she'll know how we can get inside. She was right about the fences."

Lily was silent as he slipped under the covers, still wearing his jeans. She sighed and shifted toward him. His pulse raced as her scent overwhelmed him. She was so close he could reach over and touch her with almost no effort at all.

"I can't stop thinking about all the horrible things Meiling said. How could my sister have gotten mixed up with a monster like Colton Reilly?"

"Haven't you ever been in love? It makes people do crazy things."

Lily swallowed noisily. "I don't think she was in love with him," she said in a tight voice. "I think she was just crazy."

"Did you ever think your sister became the way she did because she couldn't be as good as you?"

"Cassie was everything I wasn't. She never had to try hard in high school, but I had to study every spare minute. She had lots of friends, but I ate lunch by myself every day."

"That's not what I meant. I mean *as good.* Do you think she would have dropped everything in her life to take care of your child?"

She didn't respond, even though there was no question about the answer.

"If you ask me," Miles said softly, "Annie is damn lucky to have you."

Chapter Fifteen

Miles came awake with a start. The room was still dark and had grown cold. His eyes strayed to the too-bright digital clock. Twelve twenty-two a.m. He turned over and found Lily sitting up. The gleaming blue material clung to her back under a lustrous wave of mahogany hair.

"Annie?"

She shook her head without looking at him. He glanced around the dark room to confirm as much for himself.

Why not tonight? He pushed up onto his elbow. Lily was worried something happened to the little girl. Hell, *he* was worried.

"It doesn't mean something's wrong. We don't know how or why she does it."

He placed his hand on her back. Warmth fed into his palm like a lifeline. Lily dragged her hair back from her face and combed her fingers through the length.

"I think Colton wanted me to work for him so he could turn me into one of his broodmares."

A surge of adrenaline kick-started his heart. He'd had the same suspicion when Meiling Wong had told them all the children were Colton's own offspring. He'd realized the man was truly insane, and his fear for Lily had magnified a thousand times.

He'd pushed the thought out of his mind, not wanting to believe she was in that much danger. *Grotesque danger.*

"He must believe I'm like Cassandra, that I could make him a miracle child. I think he told my sister to bring me in; that's why she was so persistent the last time I saw her."

"Jesus." Miles said a silent prayer of thanks she had not fallen in with Reilly. By some miracle and her own courageous strength she'd escaped a horrible fate. He leaned onto his elbow beside her and slid his hand around her waist. She slipped into his arms and he settled her back onto the mattress.

Two frown lines pinched between her brows. He cupped her face, caressing her cheek with his thumb. "Hey."

Her soft brown eyes met his.

"You're safe now."

He gazed down at her, memorizing the beautiful planes of her face, the soft skin under his fingers. She was an incredible woman. He didn't know how he'd resisted her this long.

He wasn't sure if he closed his eyes or simply blinked, but he found his lips on hers. The gentle kiss she returned was slow and tender, but without a hint of reluctance. It chased away the chill in his bones caused by thinking about all the horrible possibilities she had narrowly escaped.

He rolled on top of her. She was soft and curvy everywhere. Her body melded to his as though she had been put on this earth for him.

She raked her hands over his back and through his hair. Her kiss intensified and her body arched into his, urging him past the edge of reason. Past the ability to say no.

He stopped and looked into her eyes. She was so vulnerable and so fragile, even if she didn't want to admit it.

"I don't want to hurt you."

She smiled her sweet, beautiful smile. "So many terrible things have happened. I need this moment."

He fell hungrily into her kiss again, greedily stroking her sumptuous body with needful hands. He slipped beneath the silky pajama top to find skin softer than he ever imagined. He filled his hand with a full, round breast. He squeezed gently, trapping her stiff nipple between two fingers. Her chest rose as she drew a breath deeply between kisses.

He needed more, so much more. Miles drew back and tugged the slippery material over her head. With eyes adjusted to the dim light he saw her perfectly. How could this woman not know how beautiful she was?

The more he saw of her, the more powerful his need became. He brought his mouth to her throat and kissed his way over her collar bone to her chest, hesitating only to grasp the stretchy waist of her pajama bottoms and pull them down her body.

And then she was naked beneath him, a glorious length of willing splendor he'd been afraid to want.

His hand slid up back up her leg and cupped between her thighs. She was hot with need. Her legs parted to accommodate him. He slid one finger inside to discover the moisture of her desire. His tongue slipped between her lips and tangled with hers, purely suggestive. *This is what I want. Will you let me inside you?*

His jeans had become painful. He rolled sideways only long enough to tear open the button fly and shove them over his hips. He kicked them away and fell between her legs.

Hot skin came against glorious, hot skin. The contact was like an explosion.

Miles grasped one breast and brought his lips to the

stiffened peak. She arched off the bed as he pulled it into his mouth and gently raked with his teeth. Beneath the flowery scent of her soap was a pure, rich scent all hers. He breathed deeply while his tongue flicked over her nipple. *Pure heaven.*

Her thigh slid across his hip with a velvet caress as she brought her legs up and apart. Though he'd like to take the time to explore her, his body responded to the soft stroke of her inner thigh by moving him to readiness. He stared down into her eyes. There was no reluctance, no hesitance in her face. The lines of tension had faded for dreamy pleasure.

He didn't need to guide himself with a hand. His body had already met hers perfectly. She closed her eyes and breathed his name on a sigh.

Miles entered her on a long stroke. Her warm body was tight, but welcoming. She slid her arms around his back as he seated himself deep. A low, satisfied sigh escaped her as he arrived, fully sheathed and perfectly joined. Her fingers tightened on his flesh and Miles began to move, slowly at first, until she lifted her hips to encourage him to take more.

Gladly, greedily, he did. His hands roamed over her in the darkness, memorizing every curve and hollow, every bump and valley. The sounds of her pleasure grew, as did his need to spend himself inside her.

Darkness fractured into shards of light and her cries echoed in his ears as they climaxed together. The sensation was so intense and so foreign, it was like he was experiencing it for the first time.

Then there were only lingering pulses of pleasure and the soft body beneath him as he drifted into oblivion without pain, for the first time in forever.

Chapter Sixteen

The sound of the shower going off brought him from a foggy dream. The feel of Lily's body still resonated in all the places that had come into contact with his. He could almost imagine he was still touching that luxurious skin.

But the situation was not right. As beautiful and generous a lover as she had been, he was in a hotel room with a woman who was not Sara.

Miles rose and pulled on his jeans, then sat in the guest chair where the rest of his clothes were piled. He dragged on yesterday's socks, yanked his t-shirt over his head and stuffed his feet into his boots. Lily's scent clung to him, inescapable.

Loving her had been amazing, but this morning it came with a super-sized serving of guilt. He could never give Lily the love she needed.

Miles stuffed his t-shirt into his jeans and pulled on the flannel button-up. Blinding glare from a freshly fallen snow stung his eyes as he stepped onto the balcony.

In Lily's arms, he'd never noticed the drop in temperature, but from the look of the ice and frozen cars blanketed under a good three inches of snow, the night had been cold. The frigid air scalded his lungs as he breathed deeply.

He'd hoped if he were ever to give in to his base needs and take another woman, it wouldn't be good. But last night had been incredible.

How could he have done that to Lily? He cursed himself for the lack of restraint. He'd sometimes imagined having sex again, but his mental picture had always been with an unknown, unseen image. Never with someone he cared about, because he'd never imagined he would ever care about anyone again.

Yet he did. Lily had somehow broken through the rusted bars surrounding his heart and fixed herself inside. He didn't just care, he *wanted* to care.

The door behind him opened.

"Hey."

He tossed a glance over his shoulder without really looking at her. She stepped out beside him at the rail and scanned the snowy landscape. Her deep breath in and out tore into his soul. She was already heartbroken, he could feel it. For a long moment, she didn't speak, and he didn't either. He didn't know what to say.

She finally broke the silence. "Last night was wonderful, and I don't regret it for a moment." She turned toward him and leaned her hip on the rail, but Miles still couldn't face her. "I know you're trying to think of a gentle way to let me know it can never happen again. Don't worry. You don't have to say anything."

"It isn't like that," he said simply. How pathetic. He wished he did know what to say, because silence wasn't fair to Lily. But God help him, he didn't want to hurt her.

"I would never expect a man like you to want a woman like me."

He laughed out a wretched sound. "You can't be serious. Lily, do you have any idea how beautiful you are? I wish I were half worthy of you."

Her breath hitched. The sound brought a hot stab to his gut.

"I know you love your wife. Just because she isn't with you anymore doesn't mean your love has diminished. I only wish someday I find a love as powerful."

He turned and took her face in his hands. "Lily, don't you see? I *do* care for you, too much. But I can't give you what you need. I haven't healed enough yet."

This was all happening too fast, coming at him too strong. He wasn't willing to feel these emotions bouncing off his heart. He wanted them, but he wouldn't let himself have them.

She grasped his wrists. "I know."

"No, you don't. It isn't because of my wife that I can't give you what you need. It's because of me."

She pulled his hands from her face and backed a step away. "Please don't say that. God, Miles, it's so cliché. Be honest with me, or don't say anything at all."

"I'm trying to." Miles braced his hands on the iron railing. He drew a long breath and let it out slowly. "The night my wife died, she was leaving me. She'd been seeing another man."

Lily went stone-still.

"I've never told anyone, not even Eddie. But you need to understand. I want you to believe it honestly is me. Not you, not even her."

She placed her hand on his shoulder and went slowly toward him. Miles seized her and dragged her close. She wrapped her arms around him and returned the fierceness of his embrace.

"Miles." She gave a tiny sniffle, hiding tears he wasn't sure were for him or for herself. It didn't matter.

"I'm falling for you, sweetheart. But I'm not ready. I wish I could give you what you deserve. I wish it were different."

"I do too." She eased back enough to kiss him.

He returned her kiss for two painful heartbeats, then drew away. He closed his eyes and pressed his forehead to hers.

"You'll meet somebody, someday. Somebody better than me."

"There is nobody better than you." Her voice choked with tears and Miles felt his throat go sore. "You're my hero."

"I can't be a hero to anyone—"

She kissed him, a brief, gentle brush of her lips only to silence him. "Shh. I know."

"I'm sorry."

"Don't say that." She swiped another tear and blinked the rest away. "Last night you asked me if I've ever been in love. I said no, but that wasn't entirely true. I've fallen in love with you, Miles. And even though you can't return it, it's something special you've given me."

She gave him her sweet smile, and Miles ached all the way into his bones. "I have to go. I need some time."

"Annie doesn't have any time, Miles."

"Promise me you won't do anything until... Just don't do anything yet."

She closed her eyes for the space of a heartbeat. When she opened them she blinked several times to chase away the tears.

"Sweetheart." He swiped another escaping teardrop from her cheek with his thumb and said it again anyway. "I'm sorry."

Colton swiped his badge at the entrance to Laboratory Two.

He straightened his five-hundred-dollar Gucci tie as the door opened automatically.

He strode inside and stopped at the edge of the steel balcony running the circumference of his eight-thousand-square-foot laboratory. Forty-two scientists worked busily in the glass-walled offices circling the upper level. Not one of them had yet to break the gene sequence differentiating A2-6 from the others.

It didn't matter. With Lily Brent at his new facility, they would succeed very soon.

He took his time on the metal staircase. He much preferred his plush leather and mahogany office with its gentle, recessed lighting to the laboratory. The bluish white light in here felt clean, but the stench of children had permeated everything. With each step down, the grubby odor grew worse.

Dr. Shapiro stood at the control panel on the floor level reading a clipboard. He glanced up, grinned and hurried to the foot of the stairs as Colton strode down.

"B4-5 moved three blocks last night," he said excitedly. "She—the subject reacted accurately to verbal stimuli on two separate occasions. So far B4-5 has surpassed all the others in physical reactions."

All except one.

Colton took the clipboard, but strolled to isolation chamber A2-6 without looking at it. "Any change?"

"Ah, er, no results. Just an increase in heart rate and blood pressure when electronic stimuli were administered."

"Apply an intravenous with two-hundred-fifty milligrams Ketamine for tonight's test."

The scientist visibly recoiled. "I thought you didn't want drugs used in Project Midnight. Why, starting Annie—er, A2-6 on Ketamine will render all previous controls irrelevant."

Lily Brent had already done as much with junk food and television.

"Years of properly controlled tests will all be for nothing," Shapiro went on. "All my research will be wasted."

"Your research is still quite relevant. A2-6 is my most successful subject."

"She's also the most defiant," the scientist risked adding.

Colton narrowed his eyes, a silent reminder he didn't like his people referring to the test subjects with personification. They were laboratory animals. He shoved the clipboard against the scientist's chest and Shapiro staggered back a step.

"Consider it an introduction of a restricted element. I want this subject brought back under control and performing again by any means necessary."

A2-6 had become an uncontrollable hazard. If the subject couldn't be made obedient, it wouldn't be transported to the new laboratory in Calgary.

But once he had Lily Brent, the offspring she produced would far exceed any results A2-6 had displayed. He was certain. All the experiments so far had proven a naturally developed product was much more powerful than one carried by a surrogate.

Colton turned without examining B4-5. "Administer the IV immediately. Provide all sustainable nutrition intravenously. The subject is to remain in isolation until further notice."

Chapter Seventeen

Turning away from Lily was one of the hardest things Miles had ever done. He descended the stairs, crossed the snowy parking lot and hiked down the main street, rubbing his hands together to keep warm. The icy air was just the thing he needed.

Happy people passed him on the sidewalk. Children frolicked in the first snowfall of the year. Everything was pristine white, except his mood.

He arrived at the rental car office as it was opening. Miles rented a pickup truck he could return to the office near his house and set out with robotic movements, only half-seeing the road in front of him.

The highway moved slowly even though a plow had cleared it before dawn. It was nearly two in the afternoon when he drove into Parkmont. But instead of heading to his little house, Miles took the road leading into the mountains.

After a night spent with Lily, the entire world looked prettier, even his burned-out dump of a station.

She needed more than he could give her. Though three years had passed since Sara and Michelle's death, his emotions were still raw. He was incapable of giving Lily what she deserved.

Could he have made things right with Sara if he'd had the time? He would never know.

Miles turned off the road at a fire access and then followed the path he and Lily had taken the day they'd encountered the deer. At the same flat meadow, now blanketed in pure white, he slowed the truck and looked into the forest. He thought he saw the flutter of a dun hide moving through the trees, but he couldn't be sure. The meadow was otherwise unmarred, except for his own tire tracks laid behind him.

He gave two short honks as he pulled up at the cabin. Eddie emerged, wearing a flannel jacket. His breath plumed on the air and his face was colored with vitality.

"I was getting worried about you."

Miles shut off the engine and jumped out.

"Where's the Jeep?"

"I had it towed. It needs new tires. I'll pay, of course."

"I don't give a crap about that. Come inside; chili's simmering in the crock."

"Only coffee for me," Miles said as he followed his friend inside. He hadn't eaten yet today and chili would do him in, especially Eddie's chili.

Miles wasn't hungry anyway. His stomach had been in knots since leaving Lily.

"Where are the women?" Eddie asked lightly, but Miles heard the undertones of worry.

"Lily is at a hotel in Manning." He sat at the table and rubbed his tired eyes. "Annie is..." He sighed. "She was taken."

Eddie froze, a pot in one hand and the can of freeze-dried coffee in the other. "What do you mean?"

"Colton Reilly grabbed her. His goon did anyway. We'd stopped at a rest stop. He must have found us by tracking Lily's cell phone."

The pot clanged on the tabletop as Eddie sagged into a

chair across from him. "Jesus."

"The bastard shot me."

Eddie's eyes went wide.

"Only grazed me." Miles squeezed his hand into a fist. "You going to finish that coffee, or what?"

Eddie rose without a word but Miles could practically see what was running through his mind. *Procedure.*

He told Eddie the rest of the story, leaving out only Annie's strange appearances and the intimacy he'd shared with Lily last night.

The memory invaded his mind and his limbs went noodley. He'd made love to her until there was nothing else in the world but their two bodies. Even now he itched to touch her again, imagined a hundred more magnificent things he would do with her.

"How is Lily taking it?"

"Not well."

Eddie snorted. "What are you going to do?"

Miles brought his fist down on the table. "I don't know, dammit!"

"Annie's special, Miles. You've got to save her from that bastard."

The fight in Miles wilted. "I know."

"She cured me."

His gaze flicked up. He noted again the obvious improvement in Eddie.

The old man frowned. "You don't seem surprised."

"Are you sure?"

"Of course I'm sure. You think I wouldn't know a thing like that? It was a blessed miracle." Eddie poured him a mug of coffee and slid it across the table as he took the seat across from him again. "Can't you see? This is bigger than Annie alone, bigger than you and me and Lily all put together. This is God's work, Miles. Colton Reilly is a monster. He can't be allowed to keep her."

Miles drew a shuddering breath. He wasn't sure if he shared Eddie's religious convictions, but the gist was the same. Annie couldn't be left to that bastard. None of those children should be.

"I believe you about the cancer, and I'm a thousand times more glad for it than I look." He lifted the cup to his lips and gulped a scalding mouthful. He wrapped his hands around the mug's belly and let the warmth seep into his fingers. "And no, I'm not surprised. I've seen her do things topping the weird charts."

"Care to elaborate?"

Miles shook his head. "I'd need a week."

Eddie pursed his lips. "You have feelings for Lily. Don't run from them."

Miles gazed up at his friend. Maybe Annie had given him the power to read minds.

"You have to save that child, Miles. Work out what's between you and Lily later."

He looked down at his fist as he clenched it again. "I can't."

Colton Reilly flipped open his GSM phone and pressed the answer button. "Give me some good news."

"Wish I could. There was a cruiser at her place all night. This morning the place is empty."

"She's on here way here." *Idiot.* Did he have to do everything himself? Colton took a calming breath. He sometimes forgot the rest of the world didn't share his psychic abilities and not even a tenth of the population had his superior intelligence. Though how he could forget Vincent Luggo was an ignoramus was beyond him. He hadn't slept well in the past few days. That must be the reason he was slipping. Each day Lily Brent eluded him, his irritation grew.

"If she is, she's driving a rental," Vince said. He snorted back a loogey and loudly let it fly. *Futwaap.*

Colton gagged. *Slack-jawed troglodyte.*

"Once Quinlan gets the info, I'll find her."

"I'm more concerned about her cop friend," Colton barked. "I want him out of the picture."

The man was a dangerous threat. Official investigations were one thing, a man with a personal interest in him was quite another.

Miles Goodwin had lost his own daughter. Add that to a cop's mentality and you had a person who would do anything for a child. And most likely the man had his sights on Lily. She was an exceptional beauty with an unintentionally seductive manner.

A living Miles Goodwin would not allow Lily out of his sight and wouldn't rest until the child was removed from IntelliGenysis.

Therefore, he had to be a dead Miles Goodwin.

"I'll take care of it," Vince said with telltale eagerness.

Colton cursed under his breath. "Be sure you do."

Lily made it out of the hotel room and down to the main office before the tears. She checked out and asked the girl to reserve a room at the Staybridge Suites in Woodland Park before the tears.

She made it into her car, pulled out of the parking lot and found the highway, all before the tears.

Then they came in a rush.

How was it she'd fallen headlong in love with Miles in a matter of days? She'd known other men. Handsome, intelligent, available men. Yet she had never experienced such powerful feelings. Never even come close. Overpowering, all consuming, soul-shattering feelings.

The pain squeezed her heart, robbed her of coherence and sucked the energy out of every molecule in her body.

Miles was one of a kind. His image was burned in her mind—the laughter in his eyes, the contours of his face, the shape of his hands. There wasn't a man on this earth who was more appealing and less available than Miles Goodwin.

His confession only made it hurt more. She didn't know the details about his marriage, but she knew Miles didn't deserve this pain. And yet there was nothing she could do to ease it.

She swiped the tears away. Annie was her first priority, and Lily didn't have the foggiest idea what she was going to do.

She flipped on the dashboard heater and switched it to the upper vents. She ran it until it dried her tears and ran it some more, until her eyes and her sinuses were painfully dry. There was no time for tears, but she wasn't strong enough to keep them away her own.

She drove straight through Spokane without stopping and into the small town of Woodland Park. The young man at the hotel's counter there was much nicer about accepting cash for the room.

The suite looked different, yet it felt the same. She looked at the king-size bed in the center of the room and anticipated a cold, lonely night. She wondered if she'd ever feel warm in a bed again.

She closed her eyes as the memory of Miles' roaming hands came to life on her skin. His mouth on her most sensitive places. The thick, heaviness of him filling her. The exquisite surrender to ecstasy.

She tossed her duffel bag into the chair and sat at the table. Lily took the notepad and angrily scratched out her notes.

Annie had always been her first priority; now she was the only one. It should have been this way from the start. Then maybe she wouldn't have been taken. Then maybe Lily wouldn't be hurting so badly right now.

She organized her list in three sections. What she knew:

1. Annie is a test subject in Project Midnight.

2. According to Meiling Wong, Project Midnight is in the main lab on the north corner.

What she didn't know:

1. How to get inside.

2. How to get Annie.

3. How to get out without being caught.

What she guessed:

1. Colton Reilly wants me to give him a child.

2. Colton killed my sister because she was no longer valuable, or simply because she defied him.

She'd known as much, but seeing the last item written down on paper gave her chills. The deadly reality was terrifying.

Miles' handsome face drifted past her mind's eye. He didn't want her going anywhere IntelliGenysis. He didn't even want her in Woodland Park.

Maybe she was better off going home and hiring the best lawyer she could.

Without Miles by her side, her courage had fled.

She'd thought things were bad before, but without Miles in it, her life had gone dark.

With thick, angry clouds sealing off the sky, darkness claimed Parkmont early. The temperature had risen, melting the thin crust of snow, but a soft drizzle steadily peppered his windshield.

By the time Miles arrived at his small house he was chilled to the bone and eager for a toothbrush and a hot shower. He stepped under the hot spray, regretting it would wash away the last traces of Lily from his skin.

But he would never forget her sweet scent. The feel of her hot skin, the weight of her full breasts in his hands. The velvety mysteriousness of her soft body accepting him.

He didn't know how she had crept under the steel shell he'd built around his emotions, but she was already there. There was no denying it, no escaping it.

He emerged from the shower, towel-dried his hair, and then brushed his teeth until the toothpaste frothed like whipped cream in his mouth.

Eddie had insisted he be part of the rescue, gone as far as to say if Miles wouldn't do anything, he would take matters into his own hands. Annie, and Lily too, meant that much to him.

Miles had finally appeased him by taking the keys to his house on the condition Eddie stay at the cabin. There couldn't be any interaction between them if his place was to serve as a safe house.

He picked up the phone and got the jolt of his life when the front desk said Lily had checked out of the hotel. The girl told him Lily had gone to their sister hotel in Woodland Park, and he was grateful he'd identified himself as her husband when he'd called.

The next front desk person he spoke to wasn't as generous, but he was grateful the man was secretive about his guests and agreed to "check the roster" when Miles asked for Lily. A minute later he was patched through.

"Miles."

"Lily, Jesus, you scared the hell out of me when I found out you'd left the hotel."

"I didn't think I needed to check in with you."

He clenched his jaw and drove his fingers through his hair.

"You made your position clear," she said to his silence.

"Lily, I'm sorry. I know I hurt you—"

"This isn't about us, Miles. I'm a big girl, and I'm quite capable of taking care of myself."

"I know you are, but don't do anything without me, okay?"

"I have to get Annie out of there."

"Look, I'll be back in the morning. Wait until I get there."

She sighed. "Fine."

"Lily. Promise me you'll wait."

"All right. I promise."

He struggled for the right words to say he was anxious to see her, but he didn't know how. Not after what he'd done to her.

She didn't give him the chance. She said, "Good night, Miles," and hung up.

A flurry of emotions whipped through his tired mind, but

he couldn't focus on any of them. Miles did what he always did when he needed to think. He cleaned his guns.

The smell of gun oil brought back memories he'd thought had been filed away for good and helped him out of his funk. There was a reason he'd been promoted to detective.

He had been strong, once.

You're strong now, an inner voice shouted. *Quit acting pathetic.*

Like a beam of light, Annie appeared before him. He didn't dare glance away, knowing instinctively it was midnight.

He didn't know what to say to her. What could he say?

She smiled. "They want you to be happy, Mr. Miles."

Oh God. Shame struck like bolt of lightning, bringing with it a thunderclap of regret. "Annie. I'm so sorry."

"Why?"

He noticed an intravenous line in her left arm. "Sweetheart, what is that?"

"It's dark in here. I'm scared. They make me sleep in here all the time now."

"Think of light, Annie. Bright yellow light. Think of Tinkerbell."

"Who?" She cocked her head and frowned. Her delightfully perplexed little voice pulled at his heartstrings. Almost immediately her face registered fear. She whipped around to stare at his living room window. "He's coming, Mr. Miles."

"Colton Reilly?"

"A bad man. He's outside the door."

She means here. Jesus, she's warning me.

Annie turned and bolted to the left, but before her first step touched the ground her image shimmered into a silver ripple and vanished.

Miles quickly loaded six rounds into the .38 and snapped the cylinder. He thumbed the hammer as the motion sensor at the garage detected presence and light spilled across his front walkway. An instant later it blinked off with a tinkle of broken glass. Someone had shot out the thick lens with a silencer-equipped pistol.

A shadow rose and fell at the living room window. The intruder was headed to the back of the house.

Miles bolted to his feet and raced to his back door without turning on the light in the narrow hall. The yard was dark, but light from a streetlamp reached over the house to fill his backyard with milky beams and black shadows. He silently cursed himself for letting it get so overgrown. There were a thousand places a man could hide. The moon cast blue light off the snow, but in the darkness it was impossible to determine if there were footprints or just pits from the melt dripping off the trees.

Miles would bet money his visitor was Vince Luggo. He remembered Billings saying the man wasn't a burglar or a drug dealer... Not convicted, anyway.

He would probably come around the side of the house and B&E through the back yard. Miles expected him to take the easy way, the side with the gate. He ground his teeth as he eased out the back door, hoping he wasn't wrong.

He twisted the knob and closed the door again as quietly as he could. A shadow flickered on the side walkway, then backed away. Either the intruder had made him, or changed his mind.

Miles raised his weapon and advanced on the walkway, cringing at the crunch of each footfall in the snow. His heart kicked against his ribs as he rounded the corner of the house.

There was no one there. A cat strode across the fence

dividing his yard from the next. Miles crouched and dove for cover just as two muffled shots whizzed past his head.

Chapter Eighteen

Miles scrambled to his feet and ran the length of his side yard. He vaulted over the gate as another shot smacked the wood. He landed, picked up a river stone from the flower bed at the corner of his garage and hurled it at the remaining light as he ran across his driveway.

He released his neighbor's backyard gate and shoved it open. It banged against the fence and drifted shut. Thank goodness old Mrs. Wheaton was long asleep, her teeth in a glass and her hearing aid on the bedside table. The last thing he wanted was his nosy neighbor poking her head out to see what was happening.

He eased behind the hedge of oleander dividing his driveway from hers and heard his attacker hit the gate. It was locked; he would have to climb over as Miles had.

Mrs. Wheaton's gate drifted shut with a squeak from its rusty hinge which grew louder as it slowed. It bothered him when the old lady left it open on a windy night, but now he was thankful he hadn't oiled it yet.

His attacker came to the gate, gun raised, but hesitated before going through. He probably thought Miles was hiding behind it.

His fears Reilly had more than one henchman were realized. It wasn't Luggo. Miles stepped out behind him.

"Drop it."

The man whirled on him. Miles fired. He hit the attacker in the shoulder. The gunshot report rolled into the night like a rumble of thunder. The man spun away and crashed into the fence post before sprawling on the ground.

"Ahh, gah!" The assailant clung to his weapon.

Miles stepped on his wrist and heard bones pop. The man's hand flipped open and the pistol slipped from his grasp.

"Ahhhh!

Up and down the street, lights began to flick on.

"Jesus, ahh, shit!"

"Who sent you?" Miles already knew the answer, but wanted to see how compliant the man would be.

"I want a lawyer. You're a cop. You have to let me talk to a lawyer."

"You want a lawyer? There's plenty of them in hell. I'll be happy to send you there to see one." He leaned his weight into his right foot again.

"Ah, fuck, you shot me." The man squeezed his eyes shut in pain and gave three quick, panting breaths. "Look, mister, it's nothing personal."

"You tried to kill me. That's *very* personal."

"Hey, Miles, that you?" Bernie Trowbridge stood on his front step in his bathrobe and pajamas.

"Yeah, Bernie," Miles shouted back.

"You okay?"

"I shot a burglar."

"You want me to call 911?"

"No, no cops," the man whispered with another grimace. "We can make a deal."

Like hell. "What kind of deal?"

"I know stuff. Big stuff the cops want. You name it."

"Sorry. I'm not a cop anymore. What I want right now is a beer and a hoagie. Unless you've got those in your back pocket, you're useless to me. What's more, I've got at least three of your slugs in my brand new pine fence. Nobody will ask twice why I killed you."

The man gulped and sputtered. "Vinnie Luggo sent me. Sometimes we help each other out. Said he needed a cop out of the picture."

"Why?"

"Didn't tell me why, and I didn't want to know. People in my business got a million reasons to hate cops. Said he'd pay me a cool twenty grand to do it."

"What's your name, nothing personal?"

"Charlie. They call me Charlie the Chisel."

"You got a cell phone, Charlie?"

He nodded and gurgled out an oath.

Miles hauled Charlie the Chisel to his feet. "Come on over here, Bernie," he shouted to his neighbor.

The ex-NFL player trotted across the street in his slippers. "You need any help?"

"Get my front door open. The key's buried in the begonia pot."

"He's bleeding an awful lot," Bernie said, glancing with curiosity as he crossed Miles' driveway. "Is he gonna make it?"

"No comment," Miles answered. Charlie whimpered. Miles shoved him forward.

"Ever been shot before, Charlie?"

"No! God, it hurts like hell."

"The bullet is still in your shoulder," Miles said examining his back. "That's why it hurts so much. Buck up. Be a man."

"Have *you* ever been shot?" Charlie wailed.

"Earlier this week. Courtesy of your friend, Vince."

Miles steered Charlie across the driveway and through the front door.

"In the bottom drawer of the bureau is a pair of handcuffs," he told Bernie.

"Jesus, you got an arsenal in here. I'll tell ya, I sleep better at night knowing I got a cop for a neighbor." Bernie tossed him the cuffs.

"Ah, no, you can't put me in cuffs, my shoulder—" Charlie shrieked like a little girl as Miles cuffed his hands behind his back.

"Sit." Miles shoved him into an old chair. "Bernie, wait outside for a minute, please."

"Heh, heh. Yeah, no problem." Bernie sauntered across the room, leaning close as he passed to sneer at Charlie. "You broke into the wrong house, moron."

"Where's your phone?" Miles demanded.

Charlie gasped. "I need a doctor."

"You'll need a coroner if you're not careful."

"You got to make a better deal than that."

Miles poked him near the wound and Charlie grimaced.

"Did he pay you up front?"

"Five grand down. The rest by wire transfer to whoever got you. There's a guy at your house at the beach and one at your ski *chalet*. How's a cop on the level get property like that? I wonder to myself, but I don't ask no questions, do I?"

Miles' heart skipped a beat. He gave silent thanks the cabin in Parkmont was untraceable. It was Eddie's name on the deed. His friend was safe.

"You want to get paid? You better get him to move now. Vinnie Luggo doesn't have much time left."

Charlie eyed Miles suspiciously. "If you don't kill him, he'll kill me for double-crossing him."

"Don't you worry," Miles said. The heavy malice in his voice found its own way there.

Charlie's gaze slithered over the room. Miles' anger flared. He was looking for Lily.

"What were you supposed to do with her?"

The man's jaw clamped shut and his Adam's apple bobbed.

"You were told there was a woman with me. Were you supposed to kill her too?"

"No, no." Charlie shook his head. His face was an interesting mottle of purple and green, and sweat beaded on his brow. In obvious pain, his words were ground through clenched teeth. "Vince said not to hurt the woman. He made it sound real important. She's valuable."

"Why?" Miles wasn't sure if he should be relieved or horrified.

"I don't know!" Charlie screamed. "I told you, I don't ask questions."

Charlie's face was pure desperation. His eyes were tearing and his nose was running. His breath came out in rasps as he waited for Miles to decide if he believed him.

Miles saw the phone in a holster on Charlie's belt and yanked it free. "What's the password to your voicemail?"

"Why you wanna know that?"

"I thought you didn't ask questions."

"Seven two nine two two two five. It spells payback. You know, that movie with Mel Gibson?"

"That movie sucked." Miles scrolled through Charlie's phone book. "VL?"

He nodded.

"You'll confirm the hit. Tell him the woman isn't here."

"No problem, man."

Miles gave the man a dangerous glare. "You're in pain now, but it could be a lot worse. Don't make me angry, Charlie."

Charlie shook his head, his eyes wide with fear.

Miles dialed and tipped the phone to Charlie's ear so he could hear Vince on the other end. The call rang six times before it was picked up with a grunt.

"Yeah, it's C.C. It's done."

"The woman?"

"She isn't here."

Miles kept his relief hidden. Lily was still safe in her hotel room.

"What's wrong?"

"The bastard shot me before I capped him. I got a slug in my shoulder. Make the transfer *now*. I gotta drive to Portland to see a special doctor."

"You sure the woman isn't there?"

"Look, I checked under the bed and in all the closets. The house was dark until he came home, alone. I gotta get the hell out of here in case someone heard his gun go off. Wire me my money, Vinnie. This guy charges five grand to take out a bullet without reporting it. The way I see it, I'm already losing out on fifteen percent of my pay, not to mention my pain and suffering. It hurts like a sonofabitch."

"That's your fault. I told you he was sly. You sure you killed him? This cop seems to have a guardian angel."

"Not any more he doesn't. I tossed his body into the creek behind his house. Gonna be a week before anyone finds him floating."

"I told you I wanted a souvenir."

"Yeah, well that was before he shot me. I got one arm that works now. He fell through the fence and it was all I could do to kick him into the water. Wasn't in the mood to start cutting off body parts. Wire me my damn money, Vinnie."

Miles disconnected the call.

"That bought you some time," Charlie said. He forced a laugh over his panic. "You just be sure you do whatever you're gonna do right quick, or it'll be *me* floating face down toward the bay."

Miles chuckled. "I suggest you go into acting. Your present line of work doesn't have a very good retirement plan." He slipped the phone into his jeans pocket. "Bernie!"

His neighbor stepped in immediately as if he'd been standing outside with his ear pressed against the door. "Yeah, boss."

"You can call for backup now."

Charlie gulped. "Hey! I did what you wanted."

Miles leaned close and planted both hands on the arm rests. Charlie shrank back in fear.

"That bought you your life."

By the time Charlie the Chisel had been hauled away and Miles had finished giving his report, it was four in the morning and only Noah Thompson remained in his living room. He'd tried calling Lily's hotel, but the snippy night clerk refused to transfer him through.

His old friend shook his head. "I should'a known. I tell you not to be a maverick, that's exactly what you go off and be."

"Noah, Jesus." Miles lifted his hands, palms up. "I'm sitting in my own living room minding my own business. She's not even here."

"That lunatic sees you as a threat anyhow. Why?"

Trust Noah to get right to the point.

"He wants her and he knows I won't let him have her." Miles pushed to his feet and paced the living room. He hadn't had any sleep, but there was no time now. He had to get on the road. "That, and I think he doesn't want me talking to anyone official. So I'm talking to you while I have my chance."

"First smart thing you've done all week."

He frowned. "I went to Billings. He said he couldn't do anything."

"Where is Lily now?"

"Not gonna say."

"You don't trust me?"

"I don't trust the fates."

"Why aren't you with her now?"

Miles turned away and sighed. He pushed a hand through his greasy hair. Add another shower to the list of things he needed, but didn't have time for.

Noah waited with that annoying, quiet patience he was famous for.

Miles grumbled under his breath. "Because I have feelings for her I couldn't handle. Happy? She reminded me I was still alive when I thought I was better off dead. Now shut up and listen because I don't have a lot of time. I have to get on the road and get to Lily before she does something stupid like walk straight into Colton Reilly's lair."

He went on to tell Noah what he hadn't said on the record, what he and Lily had learned from Meiling Wong, what they suspected was going on at IntelliGenysis and about Annie's strange abilities.

Noah's brows wriggled up his forehead on the Annie part, but he didn't interrupt.

Since Miles had already told him he had feelings for Lily, he went on to confess he'd had to leave because they'd made love, and being with her was so good it scared the hell out of him.

"Well, hallelujah. You're human after all."

"I'm an undeserving bastard," Miles said with a grumble. He finished with Charlie's call to Vince Luggo IDing him as a corpse. "Now you know everything."

Amazingly calm, Noah planted his hands on his knees and pushed to his feet. "You want me to come along?"

"You can't. I have nothing officially tying Vince Luggo to IntelliGenysis, and that means nothing tying Charlie the Chisel to IntelliGenysis, either. I know you don't want to be a maverick any more than you want me to, but the difference is you have a badge to risk. I don't."

Noah was silent a long time. Miles knew he was looking for a plausible argument to keep him from heading out alone.

There wasn't one.

"I have an unpleasant suspicion this might be the last time I see you alive," he finally said.

Miles grinned. "Didn't you hear? Charlie the Chisel already whacked me."

After a five-minute shower, Miles was on the road at four-thirty. He could make it to Woodland Park by seven, probably before Lily even awoke.

He drove through a fast-food window for an egg sandwich and a large coffee. He was running on empty without food and sleep, but food was the only thing he had time to fuel up on.

Last night he'd been a cop again. Hell, he'd been a cop for the last week, only hadn't let himself believe it. Unless he did something to get himself in trouble—*officially*, he was going to ask for reinstatement. It would be nice to work in Seattle again. Close to Lily. Far from bad memories.

Just as he had the thought, his hand turned the wheel of the truck into the Shady Hills Cemetery. Coming here was the only reason he ever took Highway 395, and the turn had been automatic.

Miles gulped and slowed the truck, ready to stop and turn around. He decided it was a good thing.

He drove around the long, circular road. The cemetery looked pretty with patches of snow mixed into its trees and vibrant green lawns. Tombstones stood like marble sentinels, gleaming in the early light breaking through thick, fluffy clouds. Behind them the sunrise painted the early morning sky with brushstrokes of red, gold and lavender.

His mouth was dry by the time he reached the Harris family plot. Sara and Michelle were buried beside Sara's grandfather. There was no space reserved beside them for him. Montgomery Harris had made it perfectly clear Miles was not welcome in their family, alive or dead.

Sara and Michelle shared a beautiful tombstone that stretched between their closely laid plots. The three pretty stone cherubs seemed to eye him warily as he walked up and stood before them in silence, as though they knew something was different today.

As always, his eyes strayed over the inscription. His heart still felt that familiar, painful squeeze, but today there was hope behind it.

"I've met someone," he started simply. "A good woman. I think I love her." He cleared his throat. "I do. I love her."

Miles knelt before the grave. He picked up a dead leaf and crushed it in his palm. "She's sweet and kind and she has a good heart. She's risking her life to save a child who isn't even hers." He sighed. "If the miracles I've seen this past week are real, I'm sure you're someplace good, and you already know this. I guess I really came here today to say goodbye."

He stood and let the crushed leaf fragments flutter away on the breeze before shoving his hands into his pockets. "I'm sorry I don't have more time to say it, but Lily and Annie are in danger and they need my help. I'm a cop again, Sara. It's not official yet, but I *feel* like one again, and that's what matters. I don't know if Lily can live with a cop, but I think she's willing to try, and so am I. That's all either of us can do."

He swallowed. He'd never imagined he could say goodbye, but it wasn't impossible like he'd thought. Lily had given him this strength.

"Maybe it was because you were leaving me that I took on this unbreakable devotion, like I needed to show you I would never abandon you. I realize now I was foolish. It just didn't work out between us. I don't blame you for leaving me. You made me stronger, and I'll be a better man to Lily thanks to you."

Miles turned and walked back to the truck. He had expected a seizure of pain in his chest, but instead, he felt light, free of the burden he'd been carrying for three years. There was room in his heart now for Lily.

Chapter Nineteen

"Sir, I've tried the room twice. There is no answer."

Miles punched the disconnect and pounded his fist against the steering wheel. He sat in a line of traffic a mile long. Another truck had overturned in almost the same spot as the one two nights ago, this one spilling gravel and shutting down the highway in both directions.

Please Lily, don't do anything until I get there.

Maybe she was playing it safe, simply not answering.

His gut burned with guilt. She was heartbroken, and maybe she just didn't want to talk to him.

Lily said she loved him, and he'd done nothing but turn and walk away from her. What a jerk.

And what a fool. Some people go through their entire lives never knowing such a gift as honest love. She'd given him her heart, and he'd been callous enough to toss it back in her face.

Finally cars started inching forward. It took forty-five minutes to crawl past the overturned truck, and it was noon before he made it into Woodland Park and to the Staybridge Suites on Dale Boulevard.

Thank goodness, Lily's rental car was sitting in the main parking lot. Miles went into the office and asked for Lily.

The man behind the counter was less than friendly. "We do

not give out room information on our guests, sir."

Miles got a dose of understanding for Lily's frustration when Chief Billings had told her he couldn't do anything without first checking the facts. He looked at the man's nametag.

"Listen, Manoj, how about you let her be the judge of who she wants to see?" He forced a pleasant smile even as every cell in his body was primed to reach over the counter and take the man by the throat. "Would you please call her and tell her Miles is here?"

Without a word, the man punched three numbers on the dial pad. One one six. So much for caution. Miles pinned him with an irritated stare.

The building looked exactly like its sister hotel in Manning. Across the parking lot, the orange doors of each room in the two level building were visible on the open-balcony walkways. One door on the bottom floor stood open with a maid cart in front of it. Even in the office, with its glass door closed, Miles could hear the shrill ringing of a loud phone from within. It ended when the man hung up. He would bet the room had one sixteen on the door. Miles smothered the sardonic grin fighting its way to his face.

"She is not in, sir."

"Her car is in the parking lot. Is there a nearby restaurant she might have walked to?"

Before the man could answer, a scream rose from the opened hotel room. A second, blood-curdling wail followed. Fear froze like a crust of ice on his skin.

Miles threw open the door and charged across the parking lot, gun drawn. Manoj's running footsteps smacked the wet asphalt close behind.

As he reached the room a plump Hispanic maid wobbled

into the doorway holding her bleeding head. She continued screaming, the sound as grating as a cat whose tail had been stepped on.

She saw Miles running toward her and the horror on her face multiplied. She stumbled backward into the room, holding up her hand in defense.

The woman relaxed a notch when she saw her boss behind him. "What happened?" Manoj demanded.

"Where is the woman who was in this room?" Miles shouted before she could answer.

"Mama!" Another maid entered the room immediately behind them, this one very young. They helped the woman onto the edge of the bed. The older maid continued to sob like an injured animal.

Miles stepped in front of her and forced her to look at him. "The woman in this room, where is she?"

"She doesn't speak English," her daughter said. She repeated the question in Spanish.

"El hombre grande la tomo'," she wailed. "The big man!"

The bottom dropped out of his stomach. *Vince Luggo.*

The manager shot into a stiff posture. "I assure you sir, nothing like this has ever happened here—"

Miles silenced him with a hand while he picked up the phone with the other. "Are you going to keep being a stingy prick or are you going to help me?" It took every ounce of strength not to throttle the man where he stood.

"I'll do whatever I can to help, of course," Manoj rattled quickly. He wrung his hands.

The phone sounded a shrill alarm in his ear. "Why won't this damn phone dial out?"

"It requires office assistance."

The manager started for the door and Miles urged him faster with a shove. "Move it!"

They ran back across the parking lot, leaving the injured woman and her daughter in the room.

"Dial 911," Miles told him. He stalked behind the counter after the shaken manager. "Does this computer have internet access?"

Manoj nodded as he picked up the phone. "Yes. Yes it does."

Miles opened a web search browser and it defaulted at SearchIT. He typed IntelliGenysis into the search bar and scrolled through the results. There was a link for "contact us" among the listed links at the company's home page.

"Damn." IntelliGenysis' mailing address was a post office box.

Manoj stammered incomprehensibly into the phone. "Eh, eh, there has been a kidnapping from the hotel Staybridge Suites. Five two five Dale Boulevard. Please send police and an ambulance. One of our employees was assaulted."

As Manoj continued to talk, Miles found a paragraph on the "about us" page saying IntelliGenysis was located in the beautiful northwest forest off Highway 395. It was enough. He clicked into SearchIt's map program and entered Highway 395 in the town of Woodland Park. He clicked over to the satellite image. *Thank God for modern technology!*

"Tell them the suspect is Vince Luggo and they should try to get your maid to identify him by his mug shot," Miles told him. "L-u-g-g-o. You got that?"

"Yes, I got it, sir, yes. Vince Luggo."

Miles zoomed out on the map program, found the satellite image of the compound, re-centered the map and zoomed back in. It was enormous, but exactly as Meiling Wong had described. The sixty private cottages sat on the backside of the property. A single road connected them to an immense, square-shaped building with a courtyard in the center.

The helipad was clearly visible at the northwest corner of the roof. The tiny red landing pad with its reflective-white H put the gigantic facility into staggering perspective.

Miles couldn't escape the heart-stopping dread squeezing his chest. *Jesus, even if I can get inside, how will I ever find Lily?*

The narrow road continued through what looked like a mile-and-a-half of fenced-in woodland before arriving at the main entrance. It stopped at a single guard shack, but it was no small shanty. He wondered again if the guards had started carrying weapons since the FBI had taken an interest in them last spring.

Miles scrolled the map program around until he found the perfect spot.

"Bingo."

Chapter Twenty

Lily worked her tongue around a cottony mouth. Her eyelids felt like they were made of coarse-grain sandpaper. She blinked several times to straighten her vision. The ceiling swam into focus, unfamiliar and strange.

She jerked as terror barreled down on her, only to find her hands bound above her head. She would have screamed had she not had such a raspy throat.

"There there, now." A beautiful Japanese woman in a lab coat walked over, smiling. "You not worry, you are very safe here. Please drink." She lifted a glass of water with a bendy straw.

Lily wanted to refuse, but was too thirsty. It was cold and tasted pure, but it didn't ease her worry. If Colton wanted her kept drugged, she would never taste it.

"Where am I?" she asked, even as she knew. Through a fog, the memory came back.

The hotel room. The screech of the maid behind her. A glimpse of Vince Luggo. A foul-smelling cloth clamped over her mouth. Arms as strong as steel lifting her out of her chair. The fading sight of the maid lying on the floor below.

The woman set the cup down and walked toward a doorway in the impossibly white room.

"Wait, come back!"

Ignoring Lily, she pushed a button on an intercom. "She is awake, now."

"Don't leave. *Please.*"

The woman glanced over her shoulder, still smiling, and left anyway.

Lily struggled against the binds. She was lying on a padded examination table with her hands bound above her head in buckled leather cuffs. A cotton ball was taped to the crook of her elbow. Someone had either taken blood or given her an injection.

A blast of icy fear rushed over her.

Lily swallowed down her rising stomach. It didn't matter what they had done to her. Getting Annie to safety was all that was important.

The door clicked shut. Her fuzzy gaze found Colton Reilly and her stomach lurched. She shoved backward on the examination table with her feet and struggled to a sitting position.

The cold dread in her stomach multiplied as she realized her clothes had been removed. She was dressed in drab, olive green scrubs and slip-on sneakers exactly as Annie had been wearing the day they'd met.

Colton had the audacity to smile at her as though he was a perfectly normal person, not a kidnapper and a killer.

He wore an expensive black pinstripe suit with a blue silk tie. His too-perfect hair was shellacked into place. He even had a California tan.

"Give me Annie and let us go."

His oily smile broadened. "Direct and to the point. I like that."

"I want to see her."

He strolled over as carefree as you please, still wearing his greasy, crazy grin. "Of course." He reached for the binds and unbuckled one, then the other. "I apologize for these. I wanted to be sure you didn't fall off the table."

Lily shrank away, rubbing her right wrist. She hopped off the table on the opposite side and backed away. Her legs quivered and her vision slid to the left. She blinked until the wooziness passed.

"What is the meaning of this? Why have you brought me here?"

"Ah, Lily. I admire your courage. You always did strike me as stronger than your sister."

She shivered at the reminder. Whatever Cassandra had become was a product of his doing.

"Come, I want to show you something." He held out his hand. Lily glanced at it, but stayed where she was. Heaven help her, she was afraid to ask about the needle prick in her arm.

"You're safe here, Lily. I promise you."

She snorted. That, she severely doubted. "I want to see Annie."

His grin remained, but Lily recognized the waxy falseness of it. The true monster within hovered under a thin disguise.

The hand he extended waved impatiently. Lily took a cautious step forward.

"There will be no secrets from you here." He punched a code into the wall unit and made no attempt to keep her from seeing it. She shuddered again. She remembered Meiling's warning. He was a tyrant who would use fear tactics to keep her inside. He already had—by murdering her sister for running away.

He pulled open the door and lifted his hand to urge her in front of him. Lily didn't want to be anywhere near him, but she knew the danger he posed wasn't from simply walking down the hall together.

Her legs were stiff and Lily felt like she was walking through a bad dream. She swallowed, afraid to look down and acknowledge the bandage on her arm.

"We have a top-notch facility here," he began, unconcerned with her distress. He stopped at an elevator bank and plugged in the same code.

Seven eight two seven.

Silent doors glided open, revealing an elegant elevator cab with soft lights and amber mirrors that looked like they had been stolen from the Mark Hopkins Hotel.

"Where are we going?" Lily asked gently as they stepped inside. She would do nothing to incite this man's anger. She would give the impression she was a soft-spoken, gentle woman. She would have one opportunity for escape, and when she seized it, she wanted it to come as a surprise.

"Don't you want to see where your sister lived?"

A stab of longing hit her heart. *Cassandra.* How awful to spend day in and day out trembling under Colton Reilly's brutality. Her life here must have been like a dream that had turned into a nightmare.

The elevator doors slid open and Lily gazed at the halls through her sister's eyes. *Life in the maze of a macabre science experiment.* Colton led her down a hall and around a corner. There were no windows anywhere.

Colton stopped before a door with a Japanese symbol.

"It means Maple," he explained as he keyed in the same code at the pad beside the door.

Had Cassandra been locked in? Or did she have her own code that Colton's overrode?

The lock released and he opened the door. "Because of its difficulty, all the subjects learn Japanese and English as their primary languages. Intense learning stimulates the production of brain cells."

Annie spoke Japanese? It was only one more incredible revelation about the amazing child.

Lily found herself staring at the most luxurious apartment she'd ever seen. Classical music tinkled from a stereo system beside a stone fireplace, but there was no television she could see. Lily knew there wasn't one—Annie hadn't known how to turn on the set in the hotel room. They must use digital learning somewhere, because Annie was comfortable enough with the television images, she'd simply never watched an entertainment program.

Regret sat heavy in her heart as she remembered the look of pure amazement on Annie's face when she'd first seen Big Bird and the Cookie Monster, her mouth a perfect circle that turned into a delighted smile.

"What are they?" she'd asked. For a moment, Lily was so surprised by the question she hadn't known how to answer.

"They're puppets," she'd explained, and Annie had repeated the word three times, as if she liked the way it popped from her lips.

Modern leather furniture gleamed in the wan light spilling through the only windows she'd seen yet. Lily crossed the room and peered out. They looked over an enormous courtyard.

The apartment was on the third and top level. Across the immense courtyard, a group of children performed tae chi exercises in perfect symmetry, led by a single adult. There were a few little blond girls among them, but not Annie. The adult lifted a whistle to her lips, revealing the windows were completely soundproof. No wonder Annie'd never heard a cricket chirp before.

This was nothing but a gilded cage. She turned back to Colton. He had strolled across the room to look at the bookcase.

"Annie has read all of these tomes." He slipped a leather-bound volume back into the case. From her vantage point, Lily made out *Moby Dick, Tom Sawyer, Little Women, The Diary of Anne Frank.* They were books for children much older than six, but it didn't surprise Lily that Annie had read them. In the car on their first day together, Lily had asked her about school. Annie hadn't known what grade she was, but had been able to solve rudimentary algebraic problems in her head.

"I want to see her," Lily repeated. Too late she wished she hadn't sounded so demanding.

"Of course. I only wanted to bring you here for some of your sister's things." He strode into the bedroom, not asking her to follow. Lily's heart thudded as she entered behind him.

The cherry wood dresser in the elegant bedroom had not a single speck of dust on its glossy surface. Colton stood beside it, holding a gold chain.

Lily caught her breath. Cassie's twin locket.

"I think Cassandra would want you to have this, until Annie is old enough to wear it."

She reached out and took it, careful not to let their fingers touch. The gold locket stirred an emotional whirlwind of memories. Lily had one just like it at home. In it were her mother's photo, and Cassie's. She didn't flip this one open, knowing it was her own photo next to her mother's inside.

"Thank you," she said. She wasn't grateful. She recognized the gesture as a manipulative ploy, but she wasn't quite ready to challenge him. She clasped it around her neck.

He fixed that false smile to his face again and gestured with a hand. "Shall we?"

She turned and preceded him. Lily was thankful to leave the apartment. There was something darkly unpleasant about it.

She thought of Miles. The image of his handsome face chased away the chill leeching into her bones. When she got out of here and Annie was safely with her, she would go to him and tell him she would wait as long as it took for him to be ready for a new life. A surge of hope filled her heart and gave her strength.

Colton turned the opposite direction when they arrived at the end of the hall. "I haven't publicized it yet because my work here is highly confidential, but my scientists have identified the gene sequence causing galactosemia. My top people are already working on the gene therapy which will someday eradicate it from human existence."

He gestured with a hand to urge her to the left, down a branching hallway. She skirted around the corner to avoid coming too close to him.

"My scientists make groundbreaking discoveries in half the time of our competitor laboratories. I'm doing amazing things here, and my employees live better than the average person. Meiling Wong has a nice house, doesn't she? But it's nothing compared to how she lived here."

Lily clenched her jaw as a gasp caught in her throat. How did he know she'd been there? Dear Lord, had Meiling been harmed?

"Cassandra was safe here," he said with a lilt of arrogance clinging to the edge of his voice. "I don't know what possessed her to take Annie into the dangers of the outside world. She had a perfect life here. Look what happened to her when she left."

He stopped at wide, double doors and entered the same code. Seven eight two seven.

"You insult my intelligence," Lily returned evenly. Did he think her a fool?

He pushed one door open and stepped forward onto a wide walkway.

"Life will be good here for you too, Lily."

Ripples rolled over Lily's flesh. She was so stunned by the sight before her it took a moment for his words to register.

He isn't going to let me leave.

Chapter Twenty-One

The room spreading before her was as big as a football field and reminded her of an aerospace hangar. They stood on an elevated walkway circling the entire coliseum-like theater.

Stretching to her left and right were lab suites, all with glass fronts looking over the immense laboratory floor. Inside, white-clad workers moved about, none of them taking notice of her or Colton.

At the floor level, rows and rows of silver metal chambers stretched to the far end. They looked like tiny space shuttles right out of a bad science fiction movie.

Lily stepped forward and gripped the railing as Annie's strange declaration slid over her with chilling understanding.

They make me sleep in the water.

Sensory deprivation chambers. *There is a child in each and every one of them.*

Her legs began to buckle. Lily gripped the railing until her fingers hurt. She willed away the black spots swirling across her vision. *Annie, where are you?*

"This is our main research hall," Colton said. He looked at her casually, but Lily was sure he saw her distress. The point to his tour was to strike fear in her heart.

It worked.

"Project Midnight is our most successful trial, and Annie is one of our most capable subjects. She has displayed telekinetic powers exceeding anything ever documented before. But of course, Meiling already told you as much."

"Where is Annie? I want to see her." Lily cursed her quaking voice and her inability to find something different to say. She was coming off like a mouse.

Colton was already on the curved, metal stairway leading down. His expensive Italian loafers made shrill tapping sounds on their grated surfaces. As though confident she would follow, he didn't wait or glance behind.

One of the scientists at the floor level looked up from the notes he was writing on a clipboard. His gaze landed on her and stuck as she descended the stairway.

"This is Dr. Shapiro," Colton said. "He's the lead scientist on Project Midnight and has been Annie's primary researcher her whole life."

Tears stung the back of her eyes. She bit her lip to keep from screaming. *This is a circus and you're nothing but a zookeeper!*

He extended his hand. "It is nice to meet you, Ms. Brent. I was a good friend of your sister's. You look just like her, except for the hair, of course."

She stared back at the man. "Did you have anything to do with her murder?"

He withdrew his hand and glanced nervously at Colton.

"Your sister was hit by a car in a dangerous intersection," Colton said gently. Mockery swam in his voice. "According to the police, she was holding Annie's hand at the time. Do you truly believe I would take such a terrible risk, regardless of how I felt about Cassandra for abandoning us?"

She threw a piercing gaze at him. "Where is Annie?"

"She's right here, Ms. Brent," Dr. Shapiro said. He hurried to the third isolation chamber and unhooked the clipboard hanging beside the sealed hatch.

Her panic skyrocketed. "Get her out of there."

"She's in the middle of a trial," Colton said. His voice had lost all amiability. The coldness in it was frightening.

She stalked over and looked for a handle. She couldn't see how it opened. Lily placed her hand on the dark metal. It was warm against her palm.

I'm here, Annie. I'm going to get you out of here and take you home. I won't leave without you.

"You're talking to her, aren't you?" Colton said excitedly. His eyes glistened with a crazed gleam. "I'm psychic, I can tell."

He was nothing but insane. She was certain of it.

Mommy.

Lily jumped. Tingling ripples coursed through her hand. She choked as she fought to hide the sobs welling in her chest. *Annie. I love you.*

She swallowed and composed herself. "Get her out of there, *please.*"

"She's in the middle of a study," Colton repeated. For his claim of psychic powers, he gave no indication he'd heard Annie's communication. "She'll be finished in twelve hours, and you and she can go back to your apartment."

Lily nearly collapsed. "You can't keep me here against my will."

Dr. Shapiro turned away and pretended to look at his clipboard. Lily detected fear in him as well. Was everyone here afraid of Colton Reilly? She realized her sister deserved more credit than Lily had given her. He may have turned her into a mouse, but Cassandra had still found the courage to try and escape.

"You may leave any time you wish." Colton resumed his oily grin. Lily wanted to slap it off him. "But I don't think you'll want to. I have a business arrangement to discuss with you that I think you will find advantageous. For you and Annie both." He lifted his hand to urge her ahead of him. She shrank back.

"I have no desire to enter any arrangement with you. Let us go, now."

He sighed and fixed his mouth in a firm line. "You may not take Annie with you."

"She's legally in my custody. You know it."

"Temporary custody," he corrected. "A paternity test is all it would take for me to win a lawsuit and *you* know it."

"We'll see about that."

He stepped toward her. "Come, let us discuss this in a more appropriate place."

Lily shrank back. "No."

He snatched her wrist. For such a willowy man he was surprisingly strong. He dragged her back toward the stairway. She struggled, but her canvas shoes slipped on the polished floor.

"Help me!" she screamed over her shoulder at Dr. Shapiro. When he glanced up at them, his wide eyes betrayed his calm demeanor, yet he didn't move.

"If you don't help me, you're an accessory!"

"Calm yourself." Colton jerked her onto the stairway. "You have a flair for the dramatic, don't you? Just like Cassandra."

She stumbled behind him. He didn't slow as she tripped on a step and nearly went down.

Out in the hall, he yanked her around to face him. He

narrowed his eyes menacingly.

Lily leaned away, loathe to be near him. "If I refuse you, will you kill me like you did her?"

As Miles gunned the rental truck through the trees he thought of the airbag as casually as if he suddenly remembered he needed to pick up milk at the grocery store. He shut his eyes a split second before hitting the pole supporting the length of cyclone fence. He heard a loud crack and was smacked in the face. The truck lurched over the fence and Miles blinked his vision clear as he barreled down a slope toward a small ravine. He stomped on the brakes and went sliding across the wet grass. The truck careened over the edge and planted itself in the narrow arroyo with a crunch of the right front fender.

It was just as well. He couldn't simply drive up to the parking lot and announce himself.

The door wouldn't open. He rolled down the window and climbed out. The sky had clouded over, but the day was still bright enough to make Miles worry. He hunkered low as he trotted across the five hundred yards of lush meadow separating the main building from the fence. Despite the recent snowfall, the grass still stood tall, but there wasn't a tree or shrub anywhere to conceal his approach.

A paved service road surrounded the building with widely-spaced exits leading to garbage receptacles, generator cages and air compressors. It looked like the backside of a strip mall. Unfortunately, there was no way inside unless he shot off one of the handles, and Miles wasn't ready to announce himself with gunfire yet.

He jogged around the immense building, bitterly aware of the security cameras halfway up the tall building's side. He rounded the corner and surprised a man in a lab coat stepping out of a golf cart.

Miles raised his weapon. "Hold it."

"Don't shoot, please." The man froze, hands in the air.

Miles waved him close. "Come here."

"Whatever you say. Please don't hurt me."

"I'm not going to hurt you. Give me your coat." He stepped behind the man and looked around. There was no one else in sight. "I want inside. I don't want to hurt anybody, but if I have to I'm going to make a big noise."

"Who are you?"

Miles would swear he heard hope bristling in the man's voice.

"Seattle PD."

His shoulders sagged. "Oh."

"That's disappointing to you?"

He shrugged out of the coat and handed it backward to Miles. "If the FBI couldn't shut this place down, Seattle PD can't, either."

Miles slipped into the coat. The photo ID read Thomas Lusardi, M.D. "Trust me. This place is going down if I have to take it down all by myself."

Dr. Lusardi turned around. "What's your interest, if I may ask?"

"A little girl named Annie."

He snorted. "Good luck. He'll never give her up."

"He doesn't have any choice." Miles eyed him. "And neither do you."

Dr. Lusardi frowned. "Hit me."

"Pardon?"

"Hard enough to look convincing. Please, don't let him

215

think I helped you willingly."

The man was scared. He wore the same frightened look in his eyes Meiling Wong had.

Miles clubbed him with the butt of his .38 before the man could change his mind. He fell to his knees and pressed his hand to his head.

"Ouch."

Miles helped him up. "You okay?"

Dr. Lusardi nodded. "What do you want me to do?"

"Get me to the lab where the children are kept in sensory deprivation chambers."

"I can get you inside, but I'm not involved in Project Midnight. I don't have access to that area. You should know, it's the hottest place in the whole building. You won't get near it."

"We'll see about that."

Dr. Lusardi plugged his code into the keypad beside the door. Three four two two. "Is my family safe?"

"Why wouldn't they be?"

He sighed. "My daughter is only three and my wife is six months pregnant with our second. She's... She wants to leave."

"And you?" The doors swung open with a break in suction and Miles followed him into a brightly lit hallway.

"And me," Dr. Lusardi confirmed. "A lot of us do. Helen and I were planning to leave during the move, when it would be easier to slip away."

"The move?" Miles followed him down the sterile white hall. With its smooth walls and bizarrely shaped wall sconces, it looked like a breezeway on the Enterprise. Far at the end a man in a white lab coat crossed the hall without looking up from his paperwork.

"Colton is moving his main facility to Canada. He thinks the government there will be more lenient." Lusardi stopped and pointed out their location on a basic map. "You're here. The main lab for Project Midnight is here. Exits are marked with an 'E' like this. You can't go out or get back in without an access code. Mine will activate all external doors and the roof access."

There are no cameras on the roof...

Miles kept his voice low as another scientist passed at the end of the hall. "What about the apartments?" He had a good idea where Annie was, but Colton could be keeping Lily anywhere.

He shook his head. "All the apartments have private codes. Colton is the only one with a master override."

"Where's the security office?"

Dr. Lusardi pointed it out on the map.

"Is there a clothing room where we can get another lab coat?"

The doctor nodded.

"Okay, let's take a walk. Just be casual. Don't stop to talk to anyone."

Miles had to gamble Lusardi was right about more employees wanting to defect, and if anyone found them suspicious they would keep it to themselves. The cloak room wasn't far, and Miles breathed easier when Lusardi was back in a lab coat.

"There are cameras all over the place like this one?" He tilted his head down as they passed through its range.

"Yes."

"A woman was brought here this morning. She's about five seven, reddish brown hair, pretty." With gentle brown eyes and a smile that lights up a room.

Please God, let her be all right.

"Her sister used to live here. Maybe you knew her." Miles kept his voice level as they walked in step through a maze of halls. "Cassandra Brent."

"I haven't seen her, but I knew Cassandra. What happened to her?"

"What do you think happened to her?" he snapped.

Dr. Lusardi made a low sound in his throat. "When Annie came back alone we assumed the worst. Jesus, she was one of Helen's best friends. My wife's been a wreck this past week."

"Trust me, pal. You've had it easy."

They stopped outside the security doors. Dr. Lusardi entered his code and the door lock released. Miles shoved him inside. They surprised an African-American security guard the size of a linebacker. The man jumped from his chair with a radio in one hand, the other reaching for the gun at his hip.

Miles was faster. "Don't."

The security guard froze.

"You, sit." He shoved Dr. Lusardi toward a chair.

"I'm sorry, he forced me."

The security guard slowly eased back into his seat. "Listen, man—"

"No, you listen, and don't even think about touching that panel. A woman was brought in here this morning. Where is she?"

The guard hesitated.

"Try anything and you'll never play football again."

He held up his hands. "Take it easy, buddy. We're all friends here."

Miles glared. "Not likely."

"Who are you?"

"Seattle PD."

The security guard frowned. "Not a good day for a tour, Seattle PD."

One of the cameras passed over a hallway where a man in a suit walked with a woman in green scrubs. Lily, alive.

Thank God.

"Where is that?" Miles demanded.

The security guard turned to the screen.

"They're on their way to the main lab," Lusardi volunteered.

"I need a code to get in there," he told the guard. "Lusardi, take those cuffs off his belt."

The guard turned around, hands still raised. "Wait—wait, you don't know what you're doing. I'm with the FBI. There's a team outside ready to raid this place."

"Do you think I'm stupid?" Miles growled. "Move. Away. From. The. Panel."

The door burst open. Four agents in the same uniforms stormed the small room. Each assumed a shooter's stance aimed at Miles.

"Drop the weapon!" With nylon masks concealing their faces, they made an imposing sight.

Miles put his hands up. The security guard behind him took the revolver out of his hand.

A single man in a Kevlar vest without a mask entered behind the agents. The FBI badge hanging around his neck identified him as Special Agent Marc Brower.

"Colton's doctors carrying guns now?" he asked the security guard.

"He says he's with Seattle PD."

The man chuckled, shaking his head. "You picked the wrong day to play Lone Ranger."

"Colton Reilly kidnapped my fiancé," Miles said. It wasn't a lie. If—*when*—they got out of this, he was going to ask Lily to marry him. And he wouldn't take no for an answer.

"You can put your hands down. Why don't you have a seat and let us handle things from here."

"That suits me fine," Miles said. "Believe it or not, I'm happy you're here."

The agent at the console flipped cameras. He found Lily and the man in the suit again. He looked so slimy he had to be Colton Reilly.

Their body language had changed. Now Colton was dragging her along and Lily was fighting him.

"Do you have ID?" Brower asked, but Miles barely heard him. Instead, the sound of Lily's terrified voice rose as the agent at the console turned up the volume. It was tinny and static-filled with background noise, but the words were unmistakable.

"And if I refuse you, will you kill me like you did her?"

"Your sister became a liability," Colton said viciously. "She threatened everything I built, all for the sake of a lab animal. I won't let you or anyone else destroy my legacy."

"You've already tried to kill me once. I'll never believe anything you say."

"It wasn't *you* I was trying to kill."

Lily's horror multiplied a thousand fold. Colton killed everyone she'd come into contact with. Even far away from her, the man she loved was in mortal danger.

Miles...please be safe.

"You're insane!"

Colton dragged her down the hall, digging his fingers painfully into the underside of her arm. "And what are you? Will you leave Annie here just to save yourself?"

He shoved her into the clinical room where she'd awakened and pulled the door shut behind them. Lily turned and searched the small room for a route of escape. There wasn't even a window. Nor was there anything that would serve as a weapon. She backed into the corner.

"Do you love her enough to change your life for her? I'm offering you the chance to stay here and raise her as your own."

"You can't keep either of us here. She's my niece. Her mother named me as her guardian. I think I'll have a pretty good chance against you in court." That last statement was a risk, but he'd upset her when he intimated he had tried to kill Miles. Since he'd said the words, each thundering beat of her heart was a painful strike against her ribs.

He laughed as he loosened his tie. "Annie is not your niece."

He tossed his tie aside and began working the buttons on his collar.

Lily stood frozen, horror struck. Could it be true? Did Cassandra steal a child that wasn't hers?

She shook her head, refusing to believe it.

It didn't matter. She loved Annie just the same and would do anything to get her out of here. Even if it meant running away with her like Cassie had done, at the risk of her own life.

"And if I say yes..." She almost couldn't believe her ears. "You'll let me stay here and raise her? Just as simple as that?"

"Not quite."

His confirmation almost eased her terror. At least it removed the uncertainty. He wanted something.

Lily took a deep breath. "What do want from me?" It would be better to know, to get the mystery out of the way so she could deal with the facts.

"Give me a child and I will let you raise it, and Annie, here at IGS."

She almost laughed. Strangely, there was no surprise. The only thing truly amazing her was the calm with which she heard and processed his words.

"You're insane. I'll never become one of your experiments."

"You already have."

Her stomach flip-flopped. Lily tore the cotton ball from the crook of her elbow. "What have you done to me?"

"You've been injected with a chemical compound to help isolate certain genes and exclude others. You're already being prepared to produce a genetically superior child."

Her mind whirled with a sudden tornado of information. He'd had samples of her blood and tissues since the kidney transplant seven years ago. He'd had plenty of time to do whatever experiments were needed to prepare her as one of his subjects. God, she'd been so stupid.

"You're unbelievable. You think you can do whatever you want to people?"

This was a no-win situation. She'd been a fool to think one measly woman could stand up against a billion-dollar corporation.

"No, *you're* unbelievable." He unbuttoned the cuffs of his sleeves. "I cannot believe that not once, in seven years, have you visited a doctor who told you that you still have both your kidneys."

Chapter Twenty-Two

Moments passed as her confusion grew deeper. She couldn't speak, couldn't even move.

"Cassandra's tale about her infection was true, only it didn't destroy her kidneys," Colton went on. He explained it casually, as if talking about a movie he'd seen. "It left her infertile. After four years, we decided to bring you here to harvest an egg."

Lily swallowed a hot lump in her throat. She couldn't breathe. Was he saying...?

"Research into your family tree revealed the psychic traits Cassandra believed she developed when she was struck by lightning were actually passed down from your grandmother. Life-altering trauma, like near-death experiences, rarely create such abilities, but do quite often bring them to the surface in people who have them. It's in your lineage, Lily. I took a gamble your egg would produce the desired result, and I was right."

She choked over the breath she struggled to draw into her lungs. Her heart thundered.

"Cassandra was Annie's *surrogate* mother." He took a step closer. The maniacal gleam in his eye brightened. "*You* are her biological mother."

"No!" Lily's knees gave out. *God, no, no, no!*

Colton caught her and hefted her onto the table. She kicked and clawed, fueled as though under someone else's control. "How could you do that to me? How could you steal my child? You're a monster!"

He wrenched one arm above her head with inhuman strength. Sharp pain ricocheted down her arm as her wrist hit the metal buckle on the restraint. She grabbed his ear with her free hand and tried to tear it off.

"Ah, bitch!" He backhanded her. Bright lights crossed her vision and for a split second, Lily thought she was awaking from a horrible, horrible nightmare.

Six years of Annie's beautiful life she would never know. Gone, impossible to reclaim.

"I'm sorry, but I recant my offer to leave. You're much too valuable to me."

Holding Annie as a baby, nursing her, seeing her eyes open for the first time, all stolen.

"I'm moving my primary studies to Canada." He wrenched her other hand down hard. Cold leather encircled her wrist. "You'll be my *Eve*, Lily. I've built a top-notch facility there. With its socialized health-care system, the Canadian government is much more tolerant in what it allows and, for the right price, is much more willing to turn a blind eye to what it doesn't."

The life she should have felt growing inside her, given to someone else as if it mattered no more than borrowing a pair of gloves.

The fight went out of her. She had no more will left in her heart. She'd already been robbed of all that mattered. Lily felt like an empty shell, used and discarded as though meaningless.

But the hopelessness passed quickly. The past was a tragic wreck, but the future could be salvaged. She wouldn't give up.

"People will be looking for me. We told the police. Miles will come for me."

"No, he won't." Colton stepped back and shrugged out of his shirt. "Your police officer had a visit from a burglar last night."

Lily's heart froze. "What have you done?"

"What I needed to do. Let that be a lesson to you, Lily. No one will help you. You have no choice but to stay with me if you want to see Annie again. If you try to go to anyone, I'll have them killed just like I had that social worker killed, just like I had your police officer killed."

A deep welling of agony tore from the very center of her and ripped through her soul. "No! Miles...it can't be. I don't believe you. You're a liar and a thief. A thief of lives. I loved him and you killed him just to get what you want!"

Colton squeezed her jaw and forced her to look at him. "Stop it. You didn't even know him. His death was a small price to pay for the greatness you and I will achieve."

Miles pushed up beside the FBI leader. The undercover security guard had locked in on the camera aimed at Lily and Colton as they emerged from the main lab. Colton jerked her around like she was a rag doll.

"Did our boy just admit to murder?" the agent asked, incredulous.

"And attempted murder, it would seem," Brower said.

"Take a guess who the attempted was," Miles said dryly.

"That would make you Miles, then. What's your connection to our target?" Brower asked as they watched Colton dragging

Lily down the hall. "Keep the cameras on him," he added to his agent.

"Lily's sister was an employee here," Miles supplied. "The details of her death are sketchy, but Lily and I both believe he's responsible. Lily was granted custody of her sister's daughter, but two days ago Colton had his henchman take the child from us at gunpoint. Last night a hired killer broke into my house."

Brower slid a glance to Miles. "Lucky for you he wasn't a very good one." He touched the thin microphone wire extending from his earpiece. "Team one, team two, hold position."

He leaned over his agent. "Keep recording. This is the evidence we need to put this rat in a cage forever."

They switched cameras, watching Lily struggle behind Colton as he dragged her down the hall. Her efforts were useless against his strength. The only sounds were her pitiful sobs and ignored pleas for release.

"Stay with him," Brower said.

"He's gone into Medical Twelve." The agent at the control panel hit a switch and the examination room appeared on the monitor.

Miles glanced at the men beside him. He didn't care if federal outranked state. He'd had enough.

"Get her out of there, *now*."

"She isn't in any danger, and this is what we need to make this party rock."

"You've got enough. He confessed to murder."

Colton's tinny voice rolled through the room. He was talking about Cassandra's psychic abilities.

Miles thought he'd heard the worst, but what Colton said next shattered reality.

I took a gamble your egg would produce the desired result, and I was right. Cassandra is Annie's surrogate mother. You are her biological mother.

Miles gaped at the screen, certain he had heard wrong. In his peripheral vision two heads swiveled toward him. No one said a word.

Lily's tormented scream echoed in his ears.

Her own sister had brought her here to steal a child from her womb. Was such darkness possible? Her own family?

Miles sagged back into the metal chair beside Dr. Lusardi. "Jesus."

The doctor remained suspiciously silent while Brower continued to stare at him as if expecting him to grow horns. Even the FBI sentinel who had been silent uttered a curse.

"Did you know about this?" Miles demanded of Lusardi.

He shook his head. "No, but it makes sense. I told you Helen and Cassandra were best friends. I knew she couldn't conceive. Lily was brought here in a cloud of secrecy, and then, all of a sudden, Cassie was pregnant with Annie."

"Christ." The idea was so incredible his mind kept trying to reject it.

On the screen, Lily and Colton were arguing. Colton had strapped her down to the examination table. To Miles' horror, Colton was removing his clothes.

Miles shoved out of the chair. "Enough. Send your men in."

"Easy, Miles. This is better than we've dreamed possible. He's giving us the evidence we need to put him away forever."

"He's going to rape her!" Lily was *not* going to be their pawn. He wouldn't stand for it.

The two FBI cronies stepped forward. Brower held up a hand, urging Miles back into his chair. Before he'd thought it through, Miles shoved him backward.

He turned and grabbed for the door, picking up the small broom propped against the cabinet as he went. He slipped through, slammed it shut and slotted the broom through the door handles just as the door was impacted from the other side.

The broom wouldn't hold long. Miles turned and ran, praying he was headed in the right direction.

Lily twisted her head out of his grip and squeezed her eyes shut. Miles, dear God. It was her fault. She would never forgive herself. At that instant, she decided she was better off dead too.

But Annie, poor Annie. Annie needed her.

"I hate you." She forced the words between the sobs tearing from her throat. "I'll never agree to what you want. I'll fight you every step!"

He slapped her cheeks, forcing her to look at him. "Stop crying. This is a monumental day. Annie isn't nearly as powerful as a natural child from your womb will be. Cheer up, Lily. You and I are going to make a baby the old-fashioned way."

The words were slow to register. It was Colton's crazed tone she was most aware of. All she could think of was Miles, the laugh lines around his eyes, the touch of his hands, the softness of his hair. The gentle brush of his lips over hers.

What Colton said finally reached her brain.

He was going to rape her.

Never! She would never let him touch her.

Colton laughed, obviously pleased with her misery. He stepped around to the end of the examination table while releasing the buckle on his belt.

Lily kicked out with her foot, narrowly missing him. He seemed surprised, but laughed again. Her efforts amused him. He thrived on the power he wielded over people. Her only saving grace was not to let him have any.

Lily used the shackles at her wrists as an anchor and pulled her feet over her head. She rolled backward in a simple yoga movement. She flipped off the end of the table and landed on her feet. The leather binds at her wrists tightened as they twisted.

"Impressive," Colton said in a sarcastic tone. "What other tricks can you do?"

She shoved with all her might. The table didn't move.

"It's bolted to the floor," he said. The humor had left his eyes. In them now was a cold anger that made her shiver. "I don't mind taking you from behind, standing up. There are a hundred ways I'll take you. If you're a good girl, I'll even let you choose a few."

He pulled his belt from the loops and opened the button on his trousers as he strode forward. "We have all the time in the world, Lily."

The phone at his hip rang in an odd tone. A flicker of surprise crossed his face. He pried it loose. "What?"

Lily bent forward and took the leather strap in her teeth. She worked her wrist, trying to push the length back through the buckle. It was useless. The leather was stiff, but it wouldn't be forced backward.

Colton plugged his other ear. "Are you sure? Goddammit to hell. I'll be there. Don't leave without us."

He snapped the phone into the clip and snatched up his shirt. Colton shoved his arms through the sleeves but didn't button it up. He strode to the side of the table and grabbed the leather strap with jerky movements. Something had upset him.

Miles? Could it be he was alive and had come for her? Hope sped through her veins.

"It seems our government has finally decided they want control of my facility." He unbuckled the other wrist and dragged her around the table. "I knew this was inevitable. Greatness inspires envy."

The pain of dashed hopes nearly killed her. "Let me go, please."

"Lily, darling, you're the one thing I *won't* let go." He dragged her from the room into the empty hallway.

She tried to kick and hit him, but he was too strong. Each step was spent trying to keep from falling.

Lily suddenly realized that was her best means to fight; he couldn't carry her dead weight. She dropped to her knees and tried to fall flat. He grabbed her by her hair and yanked her upright. She tried again. She would gladly endure the pain if it meant getting away from him, but this time he grabbed her by the back of the neck and dug his fingers into the soft underside of her arm with the other hand. He maneuvered her perfectly like this, controlling her by inflicting unbearable agony to the sensitive cords of her neck.

They stopped at more doors. He started to punch his code into the keypad and Lily hit a button, breaking the combination. He shoved her head into the wall.

Lily's vision cleared as he jerked her off the floor. She screamed in pain as he grabbed her neck again. "You're hurting me! Let go."

Voices shouted behind them. Running footsteps were sealed off as the doors swung shut.

"Where are you taking me?" Lily jerked against his grip, gladly risking his anger again. Rescue was close. If she could only delay him a few moments longer...

"To the roof. We're leaving."

"What about Annie? You said—"

"Forget Annie." He tossed a glare over his shoulder as he dragged her at a run down a long hallway. "You get your wish. The FBI is raiding the lab."

"Let me go! She needs me!"

He stopped at the end of the hall and punched the code to access the roof stairs. "Too bad, Lily. I need you more."

The police officer was back on duty with a vengeance. All those years on the force he had always believed he could make a difference. Today he was sure.

The hall ended twenty feet ahead. Annie appeared at the junction. She still wore the black bodysuit and her hair was wet. Her eyes were wide with fear and she turned and darted his way.

"Come back here, you little brat!"

Annie took two steps toward Miles before vanishing. Vince Luggo rounded the corner. Miles was already running and had momentum behind him.

The big man hesitated, clearly confused.

"*You.*" His face snapped to a grimace of rage. He let out a guttural cry and lunged forward.

Miles impacted him in a football tackle, but Vince outweighed him by fifty pounds. They hit the wall of the joining hall. Vince brought both fists down hard on Miles' back and sent him to his knees. The man was a giant, but he was clumsy and stumbled sideways.

"I should'a taken care of you myself."

Miles darted sideways and got to his feet. He ducked as Vince threw a right and a left, missing him with both. Miles drove a single punch to the gut and danced around him. Vince was big, but he was slow. What Miles lacked in strength he made up for with speed and training. He'd seen a lot of fighters like Vince and knew their weaknesses. They believed brute strength was all they needed and didn't refine their skills. Miles kicked him in the jaw with an *ushiro geri* then knocked Vince's feet out from under him.

Vince hit the floor like a felled pine. He lumbered over, pushed to his feet and charged. Miles dodged out of the way enough miss the brunt of it, but they both tumbled into the stairway.

They rolled down the first flight, one over the other. There was a sickening crunch as they hit the first landing. Sharp pain raced up his arm. He pushed off the floor and readied himself for another attack.

There wouldn't be one. Vince Luggo lay sprawled in the corner, his head twisted at an odd angle. His eyes were open but unseeing.

Cradling his arm, Miles raced up the stairs and down the hall. He slid to a stop when he saw a black leather belt on the floor of an open examination room.

Lily and Colton were gone. Frantic, he looked each way. Where had they gone? He chose left and raced down the hall, gambling if they had gone the other way, he would have seen them.

Annie appeared at a branching hallway like a flash of lightning. She pointed. "Hurry!" Just as quickly, she disappeared.

His blood pumped as he tore down the hall. It passed offices on the left and right and ended with what looked like an emergency exit straight ahead.

Roof access.

Miles punched Dr. Lusardi's code and leapt onto the stairs.

He heard the door two flights up slam closed, shutting out the sound of a helicopter. Colton was making a run for it. Miles didn't have his gun, but he didn't expect Colton would be nearly as strong as Vince.

And whatever Colton's goals, he didn't have Miles' motivation. Nothing would keep him from Lily.

His lungs burned as he took the steps two at a time. There was another key pad at the top. He punched the code and ripped the door open.

The same black helicopter they'd taken Annie in, a Sikorski Ambulance, was taking off. The landing pad was all the way across the roof. He would never make it in time.

A woman lay sprawled near the pad. Her long hair blew in the wind stirred by the chopper's blades. Miles' heart leapt and then sank as he realized it wasn't Lily.

She pushed herself up and struggled awkwardly to her feet. For a moment, he thought she was hurt, then she stood upright and Miles saw she was very pregnant.

A flash of green hospital scrubs appeared in the helicopter's open belly. *Lily.* Miles pumped his arms as he sprinted across the roof.

Still a good hundred feet away, he could only watch in terror as the pregnant woman raised a revolver with both hands and started shooting.

Chapter Twenty-Three

The flash from the muzzle sparked against the gray sky. The report echoed like thunder.

"Stop! You'll hit Lily!" The cottony thump of the helicopter's blades drowned him out. The pregnant woman was totally unaware of him.

The first shot went wild and made her stagger backward. She braced her feet wide to steady herself as she fired three more times. Miles saw a spark ping off the copter's tail rotor. A piece of metal flew off and disappeared into the dark forest below.

"You killed my daughter!" the woman shouted. "You bastard! You killed my daughter!"

Miles snatched the gun out of her hand. She let out a scream of surprise and stumbled away from him.

The damage was done. The helicopter's tail rotor was breaking apart. The craft pitched downward and sideways as the pilot fought the controls.

Inside, Lily and Colton wrestled dangerously close to the open door. Like a waking nightmare, he saw Lily jerk away from Colton. Saw his hand snatch at hers and miss.

Lily tumbled backward out of the helicopter. Her slow-motion fall seemed to last a lifetime before she was swallowed by the trees.

Miles felt reality slipping away. "Jesus, no." It couldn't be real. He fought to change the memory as it repeated in his mind's eye. The sights and sounds skipped like a record with a scratch. "Lily. Jesus."

"Oh my God. Oh my God." The pregnant woman collapsed to her knees, sobbing the words over and over.

An FBI agent appeared at Miles' side. They watched in silence as the helicopter pitched and careened. Smoke burst from a spot near the main rotor. The chopper made its final nosedive and crashed into the trees with a hideous shriek of metal. In the next instant a fireball erupted, rolling into the sky to unfurl in an angry ball of orange, red and black.

Miles started for the curved rungs of an access ladder. The FBI agent placed a hand on his arm. The touch shocked him back into the here and now.

The agent shook his head. "She's gone."

Miles jerked out of his grip. "Back off."

He found himself on the ground. The world around him flashed past, blurred and in shades of gray. In the next instant, he was climbing the chainlink fence. Too late, he remembered the electric current. Lucky for him it had been turned off.

He saw the forest around him like an out-of-focus backdrop, but his eyes were filled with Lily, alive and smiling. Her soft brown eyes. That gentle smile that had reached into his heart the very first time he saw it. The slow sweep of her eyelashes as she closed her eyes when she kissed him.

Suddenly, time caught up with him, and Miles felt the cold like a blast from a freezer. Patches of melting snow dotted the shadowy forest floor. A desolate wind blew sideways, sliding through his clothes to chill the sweat rolling down his back.

Ahead, in a matchstick grove of bare pine, a figure in green cotton scrubs lay sprawled in a circle of snow.

His step faltered. A part of him had hoped and prayed, but the sight of her lying motionless brought reality crashing over him. He dragged his feet through the final steps and dropped to his knees beside her.

"Lily, God, no." He scooped her limp body into his arms and cradled her against him. "I'm so sorry. God, why didn't I take the chance when I had it? How could I have left you? I'm a fool, and I've lost you."

He rocked her gently as the tears in his eyes grew cold before they fell. "I love you, Lily. I'm sorry I pushed you away. Sweetheart, I love you."

"Miles. You're alive."

He froze, certain he'd imagined her sweet voice.

"I love you too."

He looked down. Her eyes were open. She smiled. "But I already told you that."

"My God." He leaned back and shouted over his shoulder. "I need help here! Somebody get a stretcher!"

Her warm hand touched his cheek. "I'm all right."

He stared down, unable to believe this was real. He didn't deserve this second chance.

"It was Annie, it had to have been. She saved me. She stopped me before I hit the ground. I just had the wind knocked out of me."

Miles sobbed with relief as he pulled her back into his arms. She circled his neck and held on tightly. It was the greatest feeling he'd ever known.

"I'm so sorry I left you. I was a fool and a coward. Can you ever forgive me?"

Lily cupped his cheek and urged his lips to hers. "Nothing to forgive." She peppered him with kisses, and Miles laughed through his tears. Lily brushed one away with her thumb. He caught her hand in his and kissed her palm.

Two of the FBI's trucks angled through the trees. One stopped to allow two agents out. Miles recognized Bower from the security control room.

He stood and helped Lily to her feet. He squeezed her against him, unwilling to let go, but certain the man was here to arrest him.

"I guess miracles really do happen. The way my agent tells it, you fell out of the sky."

Lily slipped her arm around his waist. "He must have been exaggerating." Her voice rang with the sweet kindness that was so Lily. Miles tucked her closer and breathed in the light scent of her hair. It might be his last chance to do it.

The FBI leader wiped his smile away and eyed Miles. "I'm a married man myself and I'd move heaven and earth to protect my wife, so I'm going to pretend none of that ever happened. But so help me, if you ever interfere in an FBI operation again, I'll throw you so far behind bars you never see sunlight again." His brows twitched upward. "Do we understand each other?"

"One hundred percent."

The agent's radio squawked. He lingered over a threatening glare before turning away to answer it.

"What was that about?" Lily asked Miles.

He could only grin. "Feds and police are always butting heads."

"Any survivors?" the agent said. He turned back to them and his expression was grim.

The answer crackled through the radio. "That's a negative."

"I need to see for myself," Lily whispered.

Miles kept her under his arm as they followed Brower into the trees. They arrived at the crash scene to see one of the agents drape a blanket over Colton Reilly's lifeless body.

The tension left Lily's shoulders and she sighed. The trauma of the week's events showed in her eyes, but as she looked up at him her smile was full of love and joy.

"Let's go get Annie."

Lily was grateful for the private escort the FBI leader had assigned, but she wished the agent would walk a little faster. She felt as though she was gliding on air as they entered the building and headed for the main lab. The obstacles were finally out of their way and she would have Annie—*her daughter*—back for good.

She squeezed Miles' hand. She still wasn't over the shock of believing him dead. His words too were unbelievable. *I love you. I wish I hadn't thrown away my chance with you.*

She was afraid to ask him if she'd heard right.

She couldn't have anyway; the sight before them as they entered the building rendered her speechless. Frightened children with haunted eyes were being helped out of isolation chambers by agents and plain-clothed women she assumed to be their mothers. Many of the scientists had already passed them on their way out of the compound in handcuffs. The building swarmed with ferocious-looking agents in black assault gear and stoic-faced officials in blue parkas with FBI emblazoned in yellow letters. It was a commanding sight, even for an adult. The children were wet and trembling, and most of them crying.

"Over here," Lily told their escort. She tugged on Miles' hand. Two agents stood beside Dr. Shapiro, seated in the chair at his lab station with his hands behind his back. Lily hoped it was because he was handcuffed.

"I need him to open this chamber," she told a severely professional-looking woman with blond hair. The woman checked her clipboard.

"Are you Lily Brent?"

"Yes. This child is my daughter. Please, get this chamber open."

Lily looked at Miles. There was so much to tell him. But Miles was nodding, not appearing confused at all.

"I was in the command center with the agents. We heard everything." The hand gripping hers tightened. "We'll get through this, together."

Lily's appreciation for this wonderful man multiplied a thousand times.

Dr. Shapiro told her how to unlock the mechanism. Lily's heart raced as she released the lock and Miles pulled open the heavy door. She stepped inside and knelt in the twelve inches of water beside Annie.

Lily carefully removed the electrodes from Annie's temples and the intravenous line from her arm, and lifted her out. She set her on the floor outside and smoothed strands of hair away from her face.

"Annie, wake up, cupcake."

The blond agent knelt beside her. "I'm a medical doctor. Let me see her."

"He was drugging her, that bastard."

"No, Annie wasn't drugged."

They all looked at Dr. Shapiro.

"I meant what I said, Ms. Brent. Your sister was a good friend. I was hiding Annie's results from Colton. He told me to administer Ketamine but I never did. The IV was a simple saline and protein solution. I knew Annie was different and had to be protected."

"What's wrong with her? Why won't she wake up?"

"She's exhausted." He tipped his head toward the printouts on his table. "There were two mid-range spikes about thirty minutes ago and one severe spike of brainwave activity fifteen minutes ago that drained her energy."

Lily glanced at Miles. She didn't need to hear Dr. Shapiro tell it to know Annie had saved her life.

She planted a kiss on the child's pale forehead. "Annie, come on, sweetheart. I'm anxious to talk to you."

Annie's eyes fluttered and she squeaked. "Mmm...Mommy."

The reality of what had happened barreled over her. Lily hugged her little girl. She choked out a single sob, unable to form words.

"Mommy."

Miles knelt beside Lily and circled her with his arm.

Lily sucked in a breath. "I'm your mommy, Annie." She eased her daughter away until she could look into that angelic face. "I'm your mommy."

Annie blinked. Her eyes focused on Lily and she smiled. "I know."

Lily squeezed her close again. "I'm never going to let anyone take you away ever again," she said between tears. She pressed soft kisses all over Annie's face. "I love you, sweetheart."

Miles rubbed her back. Lily heard the female agent call her partner away. "Let's get him out of here."

Lily assumed she was referring to Dr. Shapiro. She didn't care. She had her child in her arms and Miles at her side.

"I want my red pants," Annie said, and Lily's tears turned

to laughter. Annie sat up and Lily reluctantly let her go. If she had her way, she'd hug her forever.

"Cassandra was as much your mommy as I am. We both had a part in bringing you into this world. She'll always be a part of us both."

"I know," Annie said again. She stood up and peeked around at Miles. "Mr. Miles, I knew you'd come for me."

"I told you I would."

Annie threw her arms around his neck. He gathered her close and squeezed his eyes shut as he hugged her. He gave her a quick kiss on the cheek.

"But sweetheart, you're going to have to have to stop calling me that."

Annie looked at him with the same mixture of uncertainty and hope in her face that Lily felt inside.

"I'm going to be your new daddy." He looked at Lily. "If your mommy will have me."

Lily felt as if her heart would burst. She blinked past new tears of joy. "Of course I will."

Epilogue

Six months later.

She'd been scared when the plane took off, but Annie knew nothing bad would happen. She was happier than she'd ever been before. She had a mommy, a daddy and even a new grandpa. And in a few months, she'd have her own little brother.

Mommy and Daddy were holding hands and staring at each other again. That she didn't understand, but her mommy told her she would someday. Annie thought they were just weird.

"Can I go talk to the girl?"

Lily looked over at the little girl leaning against her mother in the center row. Annie knew the reason she had no hair was she was getting doctor treatments that made it fall out.

"For a minute."

"Here you go." Miles lifted her across them and set her down in the aisle.

Annie took Tigger with her and slipped into the empty seat.

"Put on your seatbelt," Lily said.

Annie clasped her seatbelt and smiled at the girl. "Hi. My name is Annie."

She smiled back, but Annie could tell she didn't feel well.

"We're on our honeymoon. We're going to Florida and we're

going to live there."

"I'm Becky. We live in Tampa," the girl said. Her voice was soft. "They have manatees there."

"What's a manatee?"

"It's a cow that swims and eats grass that grows under water." She touched Annie's hair. "I like your hair."

Annie produced the doll. "This is Tigger. You can keep him. He'll help your hair grow back—but not this color."

Becky giggled. "I think I would like this color. I was sick, but I went to a special doctor and I'm going to get better."

Annie grasped Becky's hand. "I know you will."

About the Author

Pamela Fryer has a vivid imagination. As a teenager, she thought she'd write a book, have Stephen King-like fame and buy a big house for her family in Woodside Hills—where today you can't find a fixer-upper for under a million dollars. Reality sank in fast, but that didn't stop Pamela from writing the stories spinning through her imagination. Persistence paid off, and after four nominations for the Golden Heart™ award given by the Romance Writers of America, Pamela won with The Midnight Effect for Best Contemporary Series in Suspense/Adventure.

When asked why she writes romance, the answer is simple. There's too much violence, anger and hatred in this world, and this is her way of bringing back a tiny bit of joy. Her favorite stories to write are the ones about the common character like Lily Brent—the underdog, the persecuted, the small against the large, who somehow manages to rise above undefeatable odds to get their happy ending.

To learn more about Pamela Fryer, please visit www.pamelafryer.com. She loves hearing from readers. Send an email to Pamela at pamela@pamelafryer.com.

Between the pages...between the sheets...something's smokin'!

By the Book
© 2008 N.J. Walters

Amanda Barrington hopes Jamesville is the right place for her rare-book business—and her new life. The moving truck barely pulls away before both are off to a rousing start. It's not her new customer that's caught her attention, though. It's the customer's brother, Jonah Sutter.

From the moment cynical, ex-military Jonah sets eyes on Amanda, he burns for her like a house afire—which is what she's going to have if she doesn't get her house's electrical system overhauled. He knows he's not a forever kind of guy, but he's more than willing to be her fix-it man. In more ways than one.

When unexpected danger threatens, Jonah finds himself dealing with more than just the desire to get Amanda into bed.

Protecting her means moving in, which exposes them both to a new danger—losing their hearts.

Warning: this title contains explicit language and sex hot enough to blow your fuses.

Available now in ebook from Samhain Publishing.

She can't fight her way out of a paper bag—but she might just talk him out of his heart.

Leap of Faith
© 2008 Arianna Hart

Dr. Jane Farmer, a marriage and family therapist and the host of a public radio station talk show, likes her life calm, controlled and on schedule.

But after she accepts a package for her mysterious neighbor, Lex D'Angelo, her well-ordered life goes out the window. Now she's on the run from gun-toting goons and putting herself in situations her lady-like upbringing never prepared her for.

Former FBI agent Lex D'Angelo can't believe he's stuck on a mission with his uptight neighbor. How is he going to solve a case that killed one of his former lovers when he has to rely on a psychologist? What's she going to do—talk the gun out of the bad guy's hands?

But as the situation gets more dangerous, Jane shows strength he never expected. Now Lex isn't so sure that she isn't the right woman for the job—and his heart.

Available now in ebook and print from Samhain Publishing.

GREAT CHEAP FUN

Discover eBooks!

THE FASTEST WAY TO GET THE HOTTEST NAMES

Get your favorite authors on your favorite reader, long before they're out in print! Ebooks from Samhain go wherever you go, and work with whatever you carry—Palm, PDF, Mobi, and more.

LaVergne, TN USA
31 May 2010
184489LV00014B/2/P